To C...
With

MARIANNE'S DESTINY

Love
is
all
you
need

BELINDA KING

Enjoy

 FriesenPress

Suite 300 - 990 Fort St
Victoria, BC, V8V 3K2
Canada

www.friesenpress.com

Copyright © 2018 by Belinda King
First Edition — 2018

All rights reserved.

No part of this publication may be reproduced in any form, or by any means, electronic or mechanical, including photocopying, recording, or any information browsing, storage, or retrieval system, without permission in writing from FriesenPress.

Inspired by true events.

The characters, names, and places in this book are used fictitiously. Any resemblance to places or persons, living or dead, is entirely coincidental.

ISBN
978-1-5255-2045-7 (Hardcover)
978-1-5255-2046-4 (Paperback)
978-1-5255-2047-1 (eBook)

1. FICTION, LESBIAN

Distributed to the trade by The Ingram Book Company

*In memory of my parents, my cousin Denise,
and my godmother, Charlene.*

※

*With love to my extended family overseas
My daughter and my two grandchildren*

※

I wish to thank my husband for his patience.

※

To Vinnie, my beautiful cat that I adopted from the Humane Society one year ago, purring happily on my lap while I'm finishing my book.

※

In loving memory of my sweet dog Sadie (2016) for keeping me company everyday with her unconditional love.

※

*Lastly, a special thanks to FriesenPress and Jamie my first contact, and later Emma for her patience for answering all my questions with kindness and professionalism, and to the entire staff of FriesenPress for their support and spirit for bringing this book to print.
Thank you all very much.*

SPECIAL THANKS TO CHANTAL

I want to thank Chantal for allowing and trusting me to write the story of her friend Marianne, whom she loves and misses.

The diary and notes she kept during their friendship helped me tremendously. Without her, I would never have been able to tell this unbelievable, real-life love story about the good and beautiful diversity in our world.

IN LOVING MEMORY OF MARIANNE

Paris: known for it's charms, Fashion Designers, city of Lights & Love - every artist's dream.

MARIANNE'S DESTINY

PREFACE

The year was 1947 when beautiful baby Marianne entered the world in a town named Bastille, one of the suburbs around Paris, France. She grew up in a middle-class family. As a teenager, she soon realized her mom struggled financially with her father's salary. Marianne vowed she was going to make it much bigger and better in life.

At the age of 20, Marianne fell in love with a handsome, green-eyed, dark-haired Italian man named Enzo. They both fell in love, quick and hard, and moved in together soon afterwards.

Until one day, Marianne met Rita, a gorgeous-looking woman at a private club for "Women Only". Rita fell madly in love with Marianne, and her relentless drive in pursuing her, gave way to a secret love affair.

Everything quickly spiralled out of hand from there on.

CHAPTER 1

It was the summer of 1972, and I had just turned 25, when I met a pretty girl at the Blue Note disco in the heart of Paris. I guessed we were about the same age. She was sitting next to me at the bar, having a drink, when our eyes met. She smiled at me and asked me my name. I said, "I'm Chantal, and you are?"

She answered, "I'm Marianne." She was a gorgeous girl with snow-white teeth, raven-black hair, and blue eyes. She invited me to hit the dance floor even though we had just known each other for a few minutes.

After our silly jumping up and down and swinging from one end of the dance floor to the other, we stumbled back on to our bar stools. Out of breath, we gulped our drinks like we had just come out of the Sahara Desert.

We laughed, looking at the crowd jumping and dancing the night away on the packed dance floor, but we were in no mood to squeeze in with them anymore.

It felt like Marianne and I had a connection – like a sister I never had.

At the end of the night, we exchanged phone numbers and promised to call each other. She had left an impression on me; she was so well dressed, and her smile was contagious. I wondered where she lived and about her family's background. I had a feeling she came from a wealthy family. One day I would call her and find out.

I was working as a hostess in a well-known, first-class, busy restaurant and making decent money to support myself. I lived alone on a third-floor, one-bedroom apartment. Mom and Dad lived only a 30-minute drive away.

Two days a week, I would drive home to the extraordinary, culinary delights of Mom's kitchen; her potato croquettes and béchamel-parmesan sauce were out of this world. Mom and I were more than mother and daughter; we were also good friends.

I could confide to her about anything that was going on in my life – good or bad – and she always gave me good advice. (Not that I always followed it, but I always thanked her for her input). We had a wonderful relationship; not too many of my friends could say the same about their mom.

I previously had a boyfriend. He was always broke, and I accepted his excuses for the longest time. However, after three years together, one day I had enough of his nonsense and broke up with him. That's when I started to go out on weekends as a single girl and have a good time. Someday I thought I meet someone else, but for now, I only wanted to discover the world and enjoy my freedom.

That's when Marianne walked into my life. She became one of a handful of close friends.

CHAPTER 2

A few weeks after the night we had exchanged telephone numbers, I thought it was time to contact Marianne. I took the initiative to call her one day and ask her to meet me at the Blue Note disco, where we had met a few weeks earlier. She was thrilled to hear from me and agreed to meet me on Saturday night.

We embraced each other when we met; two or three kisses on the cheeks were the norm in France. She was all dressed up in Coco Chanel clothing and a huge diamond ring on her middle finger. I had to find out more about this beautiful, but intriguing girl. I started a nonchalant conversation by saying how good she looked. We gave each other some compliments – like girls do – and talked about the weather. I ordered a glass of wine for both of us. While sipping on our wine, I asked her if she lived by herself or with her parents? *I needed to know!*

She laughed and said, "No, not with my parents, but I have lived with my boyfriend, Enzo, for about 5 years now."

I must have looked baffled. I wondered why she always came alone to the disco. To explain the baffled look on my face, I quickly asked, "So where is your boyfriend now?"

She answered, "He's working. He works at a first-class fine-dining Italian restaurant and weekends are very busy. Therefore, he can never come along with me. He's only off a few days a week." She continued, telling me how extremely good looking he was and that he was born in the Milan region of Italy. She reached in her wallet and showed me a picture of Enzo.

I looked at it and said, "Wow, that's some handsome Romeo."

She smiled and nodded yes, her eyes glowing. Then she threw her shiny, raven-black hair away from her face and said, "Come on, let's dance."

We hit the dance floor to Bob Marley's reggae music, which we both loved. The *disc jockey* had total control over the dancers and knew what kind of music would turn people on.

I was intrigued with Marianne and wanted to know more about her. After hopping around on the dance floor, we headed back to our seats at the bar to hang out. I asked her if we could meet at her or my place sometime during the week to chat and get to know each other better – although it would have to be in the evening because of my work as a hostess. She agreed to meet at her place the following Wednesday at 7 pm and gave me her address.

CHAPTER 3

Her address was 1525 Avenue Italien (Italian Avenue). It was an area where many wealthy people lived, as several expensive apartment buildings had been built in that region in the late 1960s. Several casual dressed security guards surrounded the building. Since her boyfriend was Italian, I was not at all surprised when I saw the address.

I was curious to know more about her. She seemed so comfortable in her own skin – a happy-go-lucky girl. Was it her boyfriend who made her so happy or something else? Wednesday could not come fast enough. I drove to the address she had given me and rang the intercom doorbell. Her voice answered, "Who is it?"

I said, "It's me, Chantal." She buzzed me in, and I took the elevator to the 10th floor, the penthouse.

She was waiting for me at the door of her apartment and gave me a hug. She said, "Welcome, Chantal. Come in." The expensive furniture was an eye-opener, and the antiques and Picasso paintings made me wonder even more if the money came from her family or her job.

The smell of the leather sofa and chairs were inviting. She guided me into the living room. As I walked into the enormous – and frankly intimidating – room, I took in all the details: Glass coffee tables flanked the sofa, and the hardwood floors were covered with Oriental area rugs. I was speechless for a moment. I sunk into one of the love seats. I quickly took off my shoes and looked at her in a quizzical way. She immediately said, "Don't think I'm rich because of what you see. I'm not. I had to work hard to get all this stuff."

I smiled and said, "No, I just think you have extremely good taste, that's all."

She asked me if I wanted a drink. "Sure," I said, "a white wine will do." It was still hot outside, even though it was 7 pm, and I needed a cold drink – anything but water.

She poured me a Chardonnay – my favourite wine – in a chilled, stylish crystal long-stemmed wine glass, which was almost full to the rim. She handed it to me and said, "Cheers, welcome to my world." We laughed and had a sip of the nice, cool Chardonnay.

She said, "Let me show you around my nest." It was 1,600 square feet and had three bedrooms, two bathrooms (one with a soaker tub), an enormous kitchen big enough for a gourmet chef to prepare any type of meal, and a large living and dining room. I was in awe after the tour of her penthouse apartment. I decided this was the time to ask her what I wanted to know. I said, "Tell me a little bit about yourself." *It almost sounded like an interview for a job.* "If you don't mind me asking, where are you from originally?"

I wanted to learn anything that would help me understand who she really was and how she got this rich-looking lifestyle? I thought: *This is the right time to get to know her better, while her boyfriend isn't around.*

She answered, "Relax and make yourself comfortable, and I'll tell you all about myself. I can see the questions in your eyes." She smiled and nestled herself across from me in a deep leather chair with her feet curled up underneath her. "Let me start from my childhood. That way, you will understand better what you see and my world as it is today.

"I was born and grew up in a middle-class family in the suburbs around Paris, in a town called "Bastille" in the 11th Arrondissement (District). The area is home to the iconic *Edith Piaf Museum*. My father was the only one working. I was born on February 6, 1947, and my brother Michael was born in June 1942. My father was the only one working. Mom stayed at home to raise her two children. Because it was shortly after the war had ended, food was still scarce, and everyone had to struggle to make ends meet and feed all the hungry mouths in the family.

However, everyone in our town was still celebrating the end of the war. Unbelievably, beer and cigarettes were the most sold items. Later, at the age of 7 or 8, when I came home from school, there was no dinner waiting for me. I had to find both my parents at the pub, where they would drink beer till the wee hours. That's where I had my dinner. The lady of the pub offered it to me because she wanted to keep her customers at the bar, spending their money. I stayed with my parents till I was half asleep and they returned back home." She sighed.

"My parents had gotten married on April 3, 1937. They rented a small house to start their lives together while the war was going on from 1940-1945. The rental house had no bathroom – only a toilet and no shower or bathtub. There wasn't even tap water for many years; cold water came from a well. We had a wood burning stove, and then later a coal one, in the middle of the living room, but it heated up only the lower level of the house.

"When my brother and I were born, our parents were still living in that same house. There is no need to mention the horror they went through during the war. By now I'm sure everyone knows what happened." I nodded and agreed that I knew about the horrors of the war.

"We had two bedrooms upstairs – one for my brother and the other was mine. There was no heat upstairs in the wintertime. I remember it like it was yesterday," she said, rolling her eyes. "I could scratch my name or favourite animal on the ice *inside* the bedroom window with my fingernails, shivering while doing it. I would call my cat to come and sleep with me to keep me warm. She loved it, and so did I.

"Mom and Dad had their bedroom downstairs because Dad had to be up early to go to work before anyone else woke up. He was a supervisor engineer at a steel company that was rebuilding the bridges and railroads. He was also teacher and offered evening classes in math to people who wanted to improve their skills.

"My mother accepted jobs from family or friends to clean their houses to make extra money. When she was away for a few hours, my cousin David, who was a few years older than me, was asked to babysit me. He always wanted to play either 'boyfriend and girlfriend' or 'doctor and patient' and examine me all over my body. I never knew or realized he was fondling my private parts for his own pleasure; he said it was part of the game and that's what doctors do."

She had to swallow a few times before she took a sip of her wine and continued.

"This happened until the day I turned 11 years old, when I suddenly realized it was wrong and weird what he was doing with me. One day, he softly but gently lowered my underwear and penetrated his *penis* inside of me. He took away my virginity. I was told it was normal, and I should experience it first-hand *by him* as a family member.

"I panicked with the pain he was causing me. I saw the blood on my clothing and screamed at him to stop. I pushed him away, scratching his arms in doing so. I told him I would tell my dad or mom if he continued touching me. He slapped me in the face, and told me he would deny it. He said no one would believe me, and if they did, he would come back and make me pay for it."

I had a dry throat when she told me the story about David and had to swallow a few times.

He left quickly when my mother came home. I stayed in my bedroom, and cried underneath my blankets over what had happened. I was afraid to go downstairs and tell my mom, I had to stay strong it was very hard.

"Later on, before dinner, I cleaned myself up. I asked Mom for an aspirin and told her I had a headache. The truth was I still had lingering pain and wanted it to go away as quickly as possible. I left it at that. I did not say anything to anyone. But trust me Chantal, I was extremely angry inside scared and frustrated."

I shook my head, and said, "I believe it. That's horrible what happened that day to you. I don't know how you got through it without telling anyone! What about your brother? Couldn't you confide in him about what had happened?"

She answered, "No, definitely not Michael. He would have gone after our cousin, and all hell would have broken loose in the family. I just kept quiet about my ordeal.

"I never said a word to my parents, but insisted that someone else watch over me when I would be by myself and my brother wasn't around. Mom agreed and didn't make anything of it. She asked a neighbour to keep an eye on me from that day on. Of course, she did not know the real reason why suddenly I didn't want David to stay with me anymore. My mom would never know.

"My dad, Georges, was the most handsome man in town with blue eyes and dark hair. I have that from him, *smiles*. All the women were after him, but he only had eyes for Angelica, his gorgeous wife and the mother of his two beautiful children. Life was very simple in those days and full of hard work. We had no TV at that time; in the evenings, we only listened to the radio or read a book. These were the only ways people could entertain themselves. Going to the library was an every-other-day trip for me, so I could borrow some books for my dad, mom, and myself.

"In 1960, our dad was diagnosed with a heart condition, and he had to take it easy. From then on, when he went out to play pool with his friends and won, he came home with his pockets full of chocolate, to our great excitement. My brother and I shared those goodies thanked our dad and told him to keep winning. He never touched alcohol after that and stopped smoking all together, to everyone's delight."

Marianne had to sip from her wine before she continued, and so did I. She said, "Unfortunately, one brutal, cold winter day – January 17, 1963 – my beloved father passed away suddenly at work. He had a fatal heart attack and could not be revived by the paramedics. My mom was devastated, and so was the whole family and all his friends. Everyone loved my dad. I loved him very much; he was always so kind to my mom, brother, and me. He was the sweetest, loving father anyone could ask for.

"You know what, Chantal? I never held any anger against my parents that I had to look for them after school when I came home. I always knew where to find them and was taken care of at the pub. The owner was a warm, lovely lady. She was a great cook and loved to feed me. I was never left hungry and never did I blame anyone. If Mom and Dad were happy, so was I. Yes, it was hard on me sometimes, but I survived it all and can share everything with you today!" We both hugged each other, while I quickly wiped away tears from my eyes.

"My mother had no choice but to take a full-time job as a cleaning lady, mostly for family and friends and school classrooms. She now had to feed her two children who were still in school. I was only 16 years old. We needed books and clothing. I guess you know what's needed when going to school?" I nodded yes. I knew what she was saying.

She smiled and said, "The boys my age were all over me. I knew from a very young age how to play with their minds, and I loved the attention. I also knew it was a dangerous game and never forgot what happened to me with my cousin. Luckily for me, he – David – never got me pregnant because even at age eleven I was already having my 'monthly thing', which was very early for a child. Even if we did *it* only once, if I had gotten pregnant, this would have been the start of a family war. The only precious thing he took from me was my virginity, and that's something I have to live with. I was not able to offer that to my first love, my Enzo."

I stopped her there and said, "It's getting late, and I'm assuming your boyfriend is heading home soon, right?" I didn't want to know more at that particular moment. I knew she needed to vent to a stranger like me. I had become her confidant about her life when she was young. It was very interesting, but it also saddened me extremely.

She answered, "Well, yes, he will be home soon, but we'll get together again another day. I will continue to explain to you until you understand why I live the life I live today and how it all came about. Are you okay with that?"

Of course, I was okay with that. I smiled and stood up, making my way to the bathroom. When I came back, she already had another day in mind for us to get together. This time she said, "Let's meet a bit earlier and on a day when Enzo is working, so I will have more time. He doesn't need to know all the details about when I was a child. I only want to tell you about it, and frankly, I have never told anyone until now!"

I thanked her for having confided her deepest secrets about her childhood to me. She waved her hand, smiled, and said, "I'm glad you're such a good listener. I like you very much, Chantal."

We hugged each other, longer than usual, almost like family, as I stepped towards the elevator. We made arrangements to see each other at her place on Wednesday the following week at 1 pm when I was off, and she was available as well. She said, "It's easier for both of us to meet here. We can eat and drink and relax, right?" I agreed and pushed the elevator button. The door opened, and I went downstairs.

When I got into my car, I thought: *That's amazing that this young, beautiful girl has had such miserable moments in her life.* The story of her cousin was horrifying, and I'm sure she would never forget it. I lit a cigarette and drove home. My head was all over the place, thinking about Marianne and her stories. I knew there was still a lot more to come. That night, I had a hard time falling asleep. Eventually sleep found me, but I had a restless night.

CHAPTER 4

I went to work the next day and thought about Marianne. My God, what else would she tell me next time? It was as if she needed to release all that had happened to her in the past. She had kept it bottled up way too long. But why was she sharing it with me?

She had only known me a few weeks, but it seemed as if she had a lot of confidence in me. In a way, I was happy she trusted me. I for sure would not tell a soul, not even my mom, whom I loved and trusted so much. It would break her heart to hear Marianne's story.

Wednesday came. I made myself look good, even though I was not going out dancing. Marianne was always so well dressed that I was not going there looking like a slob. On my way, I picked up a bottle of Chardonnay. I knew she was well stocked up when it came to wines, but this was the least I could do, and I knew we would need a drink now and then.

I arrived at 1 pm sharp; that's my thing, I'm always on time. She answered the intercom, and said, "Is that you, Chantal?"

I said, "Yes, ma'am, it's me," and laughed. The door opened, and I stepped into the elevator. I was now pretty familiar with the elevator and how to get to the penthouse. Marianne had pushed the button from her end. No one could get to the penthouse without the owner's approval. I knew that now.

We hugged each other. She said, "Take off your shoes, and get yourself comfortable wherever you like." I handed her the bottle of wine, but she shook her head and said, No, you didn't have to do that. You know, I have plenty of wine in the house."

I said, "Of course, I know, but this one is on me. Let's enjoy it. Throw it in your freezer for a while, and we will have some in a little bit."

"Okay," she said. "How was your week?"

As usual, I replied, "I had nice customers and some 'others.'" We laughed. "And you, how was yours?"

She said, "I took a week off and went to visit my parents." I must do this once and a while. My mother got re-married to a man who's 15 years younger than she is." She rolled her eyes. "But he is a good guy, and I'm happy for her. At least she's not alone."

"Do you want coffee or anything else? Have you had lunch yet?"

I told her I had lunch, but an espresso would be appreciated. She went to the kitchen and asked me to come along. I loved her kitchen. I loved the whole apartment, not to mention the beautiful paintings and furniture. The smell of the espresso made me feel like I was somewhere in Italy. I asked her, "Are we in Milan somewhere?"

She laughed, and said, "No not yet." She took out some type of almond cookies and headed to a leather couch.

She looked at me and asked if I wanted to hear more about her life. I shook my head yes and said, "I'm all ears for anything you would like to tell me to get it off your chest. I'm here for you. Plus I have all the time in the world."

"All right then," she said, "let me think where we left off. When my father passed away and before Mom got remarried, I asked her if I could leave school. I begged her to let me go to work and help out with the bills. I hated school. She agreed, knowing that the extra money would be very welcome now that my brother was away training with the army for at least one year, so there would be no income from him for awhile.

"I was relieved and happy to leave school. I quickly found a job in a shoe factory. The pay was not that great, but at the end of the day, the extra money I provided to my mom was my greatest pleasure. I could keep a small portion of it, which I mostly spent on…guess what? Make-up of course!" We both laughed at the funny way she said it.

"When I turned 18, I took driving lessons and bought my first second-hand car. I was very proud and invited all my friends for a ride on weekends to disco clubs around town, where we all went wild and danced the night away. It was heaven and tomorrow didn't exist.

"I often invited my mother. We made several trips to the nearest coast, Cannes, where all the French movie stars got together to promote their new movies. We strolled on the beach, baking in the sun, and had lunch at the best seafood restaurants. Nothing was too much when it came to spoil my mother. I also took her on several trips to Spain. Neither she nor I had ever set foot in an airplane before. We had a blast and just loved going on trips together. My mom loved flying – me not so much – but it's the only way to get to another country in a few hours. Of course, we could have taken the train, but it was slow compared to a plane ride. My stepfather was also invited, but he rather stays at home and take care of his aquarium with beautiful, expensive saltwater fish in it."

Marianne stood up and said, "Hey, we forgot your wine in the freezer!" We jumped up and opened the freezer; the alcohol in it had prevented the wine from freezing. But then, you never know, after a few hours, this good wine could have been changed into ice cubes. We looked at each other and high-fived. The coffee was long gone, and the almond cookies as well. She said, "It's time for a *real* drink, right?"

She went to the kitchen, came back with an assorted cheese platter and grapes, and said, "Let's enjoy your Chardonnay and have a bite to eat." I did not argue with her. By now, I was somewhat hungry again. It was almost four in the afternoon. It could have been teatime, but with Marianne, it was called "wine time". She made me feel so at home; it was unreal. We filled our glasses and enjoyed a plate filled with the best cheeses on the market. *This was heaven,* I thought.

She continued while munching on some grapes and a piece of cheese. She said, "At the age of twenty, and after several jobs, I had enough money to move to the downtown core of Paris. After all, that's where the action was in the big city. I promised my mom I would come home for visits on weekends and call her daily, if time allowed me to.

"I soon found a job as a waitress in a high-class restaurant and because of my looks, I guess, made more money with tips than what I earned with my salary. I was very happy. I called my mom to reassure her all was good and not to worry." *In the mean time we were enjoying the cheese and grapes.* The Chardonnay washed it all away. With a big smile, Marianne told me I had chosen an extremely good wine.

I thanked her for the compliment and asked her what happened next while she was working at that restaurant…besides making good money.

"Well, that's where I met Enzo, my Italian boyfriend," she said. "It looks like when you're in the same business, everyone knows each other.

We were introduced and started dating soon after. As you can see, we've been together ever since.

"We travel to Italy to see his family every year. You know Italians tend to have close-knit families. His mother would be angry with us if we ever skipped a year. He also loves my family, but it's easier to get together for a special occasion with my family since they live nearby."

I asked her if she was still a waitress now. She nodded no and said, "Not anymore."

I was surprised and asked, "So what are you doing for a living now? You're not retired, are you?" We both giggled like teenagers at the word "retired".

She answered, "I will tell you only if you promise to keep it to yourself, just like the things I told you about my childhood. When I say this, I mean you can tell no one – no family member, not even your mother or friends. Do I have your word, Chantal?"

I said, "Yes, of course. If that's what you want, it's a promise." The adrenaline was now flowing fast in my veins, and my heart was pounding. *Why did she want me to keep this a secret? Work was work; what could be so secret about it? What was she about to tell me, that no one should know about? And why did she want me to know? Was it just because I had asked her what she did for a living?* Well, I was about to know another secret.

She curled her feet up beneath her in one of her leather chairs, took a sip of her wine, and said, "What I am about to tell you will either be received with disgust, and you'll run away, or you will understand and stay my friend. It's as simple as that!"

I smiled. "It can't be so bad that I'll have to run out of here, can it?"

She shrugged her shoulders and said jokingly, "Maybe…you'll be the judge." She then told me she had wanted to get out of the restaurant business; it was too hectic and stressful. "Enzo was making good money.

He loved the restaurant business because he was a chef at heart, but I was due for something else.

"One day, I saw an ad in the paper. They were looking for ladies and young girls who were willing to make good money by accompanying businessmen out to dinner while they were in town for a short stay. I spoke to Enzo about it. He said, 'Just go for it. Check it out, and see what it's all about.' I called the phone number from the ad, and got a lady on the phone. She spoke in a well-mannered voice and invited me to meet with her, which I did.

"The location I was given was situated deep in the woods just outside the core of downtown Paris. I arrived at a huge mansion named 'Topaz'. It had a driveway for limousines and parking space all the way around the house. I couldn't believe my eyes. I thought it looked like a castle and wondered what was waiting for me inside. A young man who looked like a bodybuilder escorted me in. Then I waited patiently for Ginette the owner in the hallway, which featured a marble floor that looked like it had been custom-made for this mansion.

"Ginette showed up a few minutes later and greeted me warmly. She invited me into her 'office' and asked me to take a seat. She was very polite. She asked me if I wanted a drink or coffee or tea. I agreed and took the coffee. I needed the caffeine because I felt extremely nervous. She picked up the phone, and asked someone to bring two coffees with milk and sugar on the side to her interview office.

"Two minutes later, a beautiful girl came in with the coffees on a silver tray, accompanied by a plate of cookies and chocolate. *What service*, I thought, while observing the lady of the house, who seemed to have it all under control."

My mouth was dry from listening to Marianne's story, and I poured some more wine into my glass. She laughed. "What's the matter, Chantal? You're very thirsty all of a sudden!"

I blushed. "Yes I am. It's so exciting hearing you tell me all this." I waved my hand. "But please continue if there is more!"

She continued. "Without hesitation, Ginette told me what the job was about. 'First of all, she said, "this is a private club. Men and woman alike have to become members to get into the club. Your job, Marianne, would be to entertain the customers when they come in to have a chat. They are from all walks of life: lawyers, doctors, and politicians.

"Ginette said, 'The customer has the right to pick and choose with whom he wants to have a conversation. The waiting area is very large, so all the girls are sitting on one of the sofas, reading books and magazines. You just have to look up and welcome each client when he walks in so he can have a look at you and decide with whom he wants to have a drink and conversation. Do you understand the concept, Marianne?' I nodded.

"'I have, at this given moment, nine girls working for me. If you accept this job, I will introduce you later.'"

I stopped Marianne right there, and asked, "What kind of job was this, just having conversations with the clients?" I had a vague idea what was to come, but I wanted to hear it from her.

Marianne looked at me and smiled. "I knew you were going to ask me this. Just let me continue with what happened after Ginette told me what kind of money I would make, if I accepted the 'job'.

"I told Ginette that I was somewhat reluctant based on the job description and needed to know more about exactly what the customers would expect from the 'girls'.

"She said, 'Well they will offer you a drink. They sometimes order a bottle of champagne, but I have to warn you, if you feel you're getting drunk, throw the drink into the ice bucket when the customer leaves for the bathroom. I don't want any of my girls to be drunk or get sick.'

"'On some occasions, the clients want more than just a conversation if they like you. If you agree and like him as well, you may invite him into one of our luxury bedroom suites and continue in private. After a while, and only if you want to, you may end up having sex. If that's the case, you will earn around $300 for your service plus tips if any. Normally you would spend about one hour together with the customer. Also, you may choose your days and hours you want to work, as long as you show up at the time you are scheduled to work or let me know a day in advance if you can't make it. How does that sound Marianne?'

"Ginette looked at me with some glitter of hope that I would accept her offer right away. However, I still had to digest the 'job' description. Let me tell you, Chantal, I had to make a decision right then and there. It all sounded good: I could choose my own hours, and the money I could make was unbelievable. The question was if would Enzo be okay with it and if I could do it?

"So, I told Ginette that I would get back to her the next day. I needed time to think this over. She told me she needed an answer as soon as possible. She had other girls lined up for the job and had to decide soon. But she added that she liked me a lot and that I was very attractive and beautiful. She was certain I would make a lot of money if I joined her 'club.'"

I needed a break and had to stand up to stretch my legs. We both stood up and walked around, looking out the window. I looked at Marianne and said, "My God, that sounds good money-wise. But were you sure you could handle that kind of work, and what did Enzo say when you told him?"

Marianne said, "Enzo thought I should give it a try – as long, as there was no sex involved, which was something, as you can imagine, he did not like at all. He knew my heart belonged to him. Sex was not to happen if I could avoid it, he said, and if it had to happen, I should always use protection. I would have to stop the job immediately if the customers requested sex too often. I totally agreed with him."

I was speechless: Her boyfriend agreed with her entertaining men at a private club, only if there was not too much sex involved? Sure, she would bring lots of money to their bank account, and she could pick and choose the customer and choose the hours and days. It all sounded good. No wonder she couldn't tell any of her family what her "occupation" was.

We sat down again. She said, "After careful consideration, I accepted the job, but I will tell you more about it later." She continued, "I had one of the first breast implant operations ever done here."

My mouth fell wide open, and I just nodded yes.

She said, "Here in France, it was just on the market and in its early stages. So I had 'them' done – not overly big, just enough to improve on my own breasts. I wanted to look good."

Then suddenly, she lifted her blouse and showed me tiny, almost invisible, scars underneath her breasts. I must admit she had a beautiful body. I could see the curves of her waist, and just for a second, I knew every man would want to have this girl all to himself at the private club. She was not at all shy to show me her breasts, after all, we were both woman. Maybe by now she was used to showing her breasts to her customers. I wasn't sure how long she had been in this well paying "job".

I felt a bit uncomfortable though. She was more than outgoing. It did not seem to bother her to lift her clothing without warning or ask me if I would like to see her boob job. Then she asked me if I would like to touch them and feel how firm they were. She was still holding her blouse up and exposing her breasts. I hesitated for a second, but I did not want to disappoint her, so I moved my hand to touch one of her breasts. To tell you the truth, it felt like concrete and not real compared to my own breasts. I told her that they felt I a lot firmer than mine! We both laughed out loud. We were now a little tipsy. It was around six o'clock.

I asked her for a glass of water; we both needed something other than wine. We both walked to the kitchen, and she poured me a large glass of water. She opened the fridge and took out some smoked salmon and some crackers, and we walked back to her living room.

"So, you accepted the job, but are you still working there?" I asked.

She nodded yes, and said, "You know, Chantal, when you are in that kind of 'business', it's hard to go elsewhere. The money alone will keep you going. When I'm not working at Topaz, just for fun, I will go to the avenue where all the street hookers walk up and down." She laughed. "Actually, I just like to see how the 'girls' on the street approach the men out there."

I told her, she was playing with fire; those girls might have a pimp waiting at the corner. I thought Marianne's "fun" sounded dangerous.

I sat there on her couch, my eyes wide open, looking at a beautiful girl who still had a long life ahead of her and was taking unnecessary risks. She could end up dead in an alley, while she was making tons of money elsewhere in a somewhat safer place. What was she thinking? How did this all come to life? Why did she enter this weird adventure to make money from entertaining men?

She could see the worried expression on my face. I was in disbelief, especially about the last story on the streets – and just for fun, for heaven sakes. "Don't worry," she said. "I don't do that often, only when I'm bored. It has been a while since I've been there, and I probably will stop going all together. I've lost interest and the energy somewhat. Also, Enzo doesn't know anything about this; he would be very upset with me if he knew.

"I'm usually at Topaz a few days a week, where I make between $200 and $400 a night. I never stay too long. There's no need. When I'm fed up with their nonsense, I'm out. I can only handle two or three regular customers a night and listen to their stories and lies.

I answered, "So, I assume you are only doing this for the money. Is Enzo okay with that? How does he know when there is sex involved and when there isn't?"

"Well, Chantal, men don't need to know everything, right? I lie occasionally to keep the suspicion away. Besides, he has no choice. He loves our luxury way of living and believes I have safe sex the few times it happens. I don't want to end up with a disease or become pregnant. And by the way, we do love each other; he has nothing to worry about. I love him to the moon and back.

"Enzo makes good money too, being the most handsome and charming waiter at the restaurant. However, he can't compete with what I bring to our bank account."

While sipping my drink, I thought: *Who in the world makes that kind of money?* I had assumed that bordellos had gone out of business long ago; they belonged to the 1800s era or the early 1920s. But from what I had just heard, that was not so. Only in this day and age, they called them "private clubs" with a mandatory membership fee.

From what I could gather, these kinds of private clubs were a hell of an operation. They were successful, profit-making businesses, with elegant and high-ranking, rich customers and the most beautiful girls on the market.

Marianne took a brief pause to fill our empty glasses and popped a piece of cheese in her mouth. She then said, "This private club is the most secure place for us girls to work. If we worked as a call girl for an escort service, we would have to go where the client wanted us to go. That's risky business; I would never do that. You know what I mean, Chantal?"

I nodded yes but thought: *In my wildest dreams, I could never do what you are doing. No, I don't know what you mean.* I just pretended I understood.

Marianne continued. She said the club Topaz had several advantages. "It has a luxurious, superior quality interior – very French with a hint of mystery. I like it there and most of the girls do. Some have a boyfriend or a hubby; a few are single. We do what we want with the money, and don't have to worry about some pimp waiting on the corner of the street to take our money. Yes, my boyfriend knows what kind of work I do, but we have a normal life, and there is never talk about, 'How was your day'. Enzo never asks me anything about Topaz. We love each other and are a happy couple with a good bank account, which keeps growing.

"Although escort services are technically legal, we at the club are sometimes raided by police and forced to go home that night. It's only temporary, so we can protect ourselves from being arrested.

"As we see it, we are making people happy without hurting anyone. We consider ourselves as well-educated girls, and by the same token, we enjoy the opportunity to make a good income for our families in just a few hours a week."

I sat there very quietly, listening to Marianne, who laid out everything she wanted me to know in detail without even feeling a bit uncomfortable with her story or job description. I excused myself and headed to the bathroom. The wine had gotten to me and so had the detailed story about "making people happy without hurting anyone". My head was all over the place. What a situation, and it seemed as if she was only halfway through her story, from what I could gather.

When I came back, she looked at me and said, "Are you okay, my friend? Should I continue? Are you up to hearing more, Chantal?"

I said, "Yes, of course, I'm all yours until it's time to go home." We laughed, stretched our legs, and continued the conversation.

Marianne said, "When I joined Topaz, I had long conversations with Enzo about it, as you can imagine. I had to promise him I would never leave him for another man or have unprotected sex. That promise I will keep forever, I told him, and by the way, we are too much in love for that to happen.

"When he saw me walk out the first day, I looked like a business executive on my way to an important meeting. I had just enough make-up around my eyes to make them a more piercing blue. Underneath my handsome suit, however, I had the most expensive matching set of lingerie on – bra, panties. This soon became the trademark for all the girls. The colours were mostly pink- baby blue, or yellow –anything but white.

"The customers found us irresistible, dressed as executives. And if it went that far, we would head off to one of the luxury suites. When they saw this beautiful underwear, they were breathless at times. This made it more pleasant for us. The more excited the customer is, the easier things are when it comes down to the nitty-gritty.

"When I told Enzo about this, he said, 'One day I will pop in and be your customer. Watch out girl.' But so far, he never has and never will." We both laughed hard at that.

It was now around 8:30 pm. I asked when Enzo was coming home.

"Oh, not before midnight or 1 am," Marianne answered.

I let out a sigh of relief because I wanted to know more. She smiled and said, "Don't worry, we have plenty of time. I'm sure you are interested to hear more about my exciting life, right?"

I nodded. *"Exciting," she said. Was it ever...*

She first headed to the kitchen and said, "Before I continue, let's have a bite to eat." She opened her fridge in her enormous kitchen and brought out a plate of Brie cheese. We still had smoked salmon. She heated up a French baguette in the oven for a few minutes, chopped up some onion and parsley, and placed it all on a plate on her glass-top dinner table. She waved at me to join her. "This should do just fine with our leftover Chardonnay, don't you agree?" she said.

I agreed. I was now starving for real food and took a bite into the warm, crunchy French bread. I topped it with butter, poured a bit of salt on it (a family habit), and devoured it with a piece of Brie cheese in seconds. The smoked salmon came next; I rolled it up with onion, parsley, and a few capers. It was exquisite.

We chatted mostly about how hungry we were after all the storytelling and about the quality of the food we were devouring with the wine. This meal was wonderful. Marianne knew how to be a hostess at home; she must have done this many times before, I guessed.

After about 30-45 minutes or so, we slowly returned to our seats in the living room. I asked her for a glass of ice water. She smiled and said, "Yes, I know you still have to drive home, plus you want to stay focused to hear more about me, don't you?"

"Yep, you got that right," I said, jokingly. "So, Marianne, tell me what exactly are the days and hours you 'work' at that place?"

She answered, "First of all, we're open from 3 pm till 1 am on weekdays, and on Saturdays we're open from 6 pm till midnight. Topaz is closed on Sundays when most clients are with their significant others." She laughed. "Since I can choose my days to work, I take the days off when Enzo has his day off. That way, at least we see each other on a normal time of the day and can spend some quality time together.

"I alternate my day off every other week on Saturday. That way, I can go out dancing and shake off all the weird stuff that some clients leave me thinking about. My boss, Ginette, needs to know one week in advance when we want our days off. Having said that, I only work 2-3 days a week for 2 or 3 hours because with the hourly rate we charge, there is no need to work longer.

"Even without sex, after a few hours of conversation with men about their life and marital problems, that's about all we can take. We feel like a priest sometimes. We're the only ones to whom those men can unburden all their personal problems." We both laughed hysterically.

"The only thing that bugs me sometimes is that we always have to be dressed up; high heels are mandatory. It looks sexy, and the sexier we look, the better we will be treated. Plus, we will get a bigger tip on top of what the customer already paid. Ginette always says that if you act like a lady, you'll be treated like one.

"And then of course, the lady of the house, Ginette (we call her Gina between the girls), is very protective of us. For example, if you have a cold, there is no need to show up. If you have your monthly 'thing', you don't need to show up either (which I automatically wouldn't do anyway). I'm not that desperate for the money. She cooks for all of us. Every girl takes their turn to eat; only a few of the girls need to be on standby for unexpected guests.

"Gina – I will call her Gina from now on – is a wonderful cook. The only ingredients she never puts into her food are garlic and onions – just what I like so much." Marianne sighed, and we both started laughing.

I said, "Silly Marianne, of course Gina doesn't want to use garlic or onion. Who would want to have a conversation with you when you smell like an onion?" We both laughed and made jokes about smelly breath.

Then I asked her bluntly, "Do you use your own name at work?"

She shook her head. "No, of course not. What I do for a living is a fantasy world. I call myself "Margot", after Margot Hemingway. I always liked that name. Do you like it?"

I said, "Yes, I like it. But I can call you Marianne, right?"

She said, "Of course, you're not a 'customer'. We're friends, and not just any friends. I consider you as one of my best friends, all right!"

She blew me a kiss from the other sofa in front of me; it made me blush a bit. "I always giggle inside," she said, "when men try to find out what my real name is or where I come from or start speculating about my life outside my work. Customers always try and analyze the true motives for working in this business. I always make it clear and simple. I tell them it's because 'I hate being poor more than I hate sin, then they are silent.

"We, the girls, all signed up to make money. Although some single girls are looking for adventure. A few even claim they are doing it for the sex only, which I doubt. At Topaz, I think we are one of the highest paid in the area, if not in the country, and have the wealthiest clients. In this business, we make more money than with any other job out there and twice or three times more than being a waitress. I know because I was a waitress before."

I was mesmerized by everything I was hearing, but she kept going and added, "This kind of sex trade was never discussed at home when I was a child. This was a business no one ever talked about, but my family members all knew it existed.

"My way of thinking is that if no one forces you to do what you don't like and if some men are willing to pay for you to have sex with them and a few conversations, then I don't see anything wrong with it. If you play it safe for everyone involved, there's nothing wrong with what I do."

I sat there listening to Marianne's matter-of-fact stories and thought: *My goodness, this sounds like any other commodity. It's the law of supply and demand. It was almost like selling your body to whoever was willing to buy it, with no questions asked.*

When she was quiet for a minute, I said, "Do any of your family members ever ask you what job you do?"

Marianne responded quickly. "Of course not. They don't know anything. I have a hard time lying to my mom and stepdad and my brother, who is always trying to figure out what I do for a living.

"When my brother comes down and see all these expensive things in my home, I always tell him that Enzo makes a lot of money. He believes me, and he's okay with that. Also, some of my friends wonder why Enzo and I have such a different schedule. But I would like to keep this a secret as long as possible. Chantal, you promised not to tell anyone right?"

I looked at her pretty face and said, "You have my word, Marianne. Whatever you do and told me is locked in a little corner of my brain, and my lips are sealed, except for a glass of Chardonnay…"

We both smiled. She leaned over and hugged me like a schoolgirl, kissing me on the cheek and slightly on my lips. She said, "You're a wonderful person, Chantal. I'm glad I met you and that you're my friend."

It was now almost 11 pm. I said, "Marianne, as much as I would like to stay and listen to your business adventures, I've got to go. I am working tomorrow." I slowly got up off her soft leather sofa and asked if I could give her a hand with the dishes.

She said, "No, that's alright. I will do this and wait for Enzo to arrive. He will want to kick off his shoes and relax before we go to bed. Don't worry. I'm glad you came, and stay in touch, okay?"

We hugged each other. She escorted me to the elevator and waved at me before the doors closed. While walking to my car, I thought: *Such a beautiful girl. Why on earth is she in this kind of business?* Even more mind-boggling was why her boyfriend was allowing her to do this. I could not wrap my head around it, and frankly, it was none of my business either. I just thought it was a shame and felt somewhat sorry for her.

CHAPTER 5

Two days later, Marianne called me and asked if I was free Friday afternoon. I said, "Well, I can take that day off, if you want. What's up?"

She told me, "You should meet Enzo. He's preparing real Italian food, made by a real Italian." She giggled when she said this. "Then after dinner, around 5 pm, he leaves for work. Plus, he is eager to meet you since I talk so much about you. Will that work for you?"

I gladly accepted this unexpected dinner invitation and the chance to see her boyfriend, who would cook for all of us. I told her, "I'll be there by 4 pm." She was glad to hear I would attend and finally meet Enzo, her man of more than 5 years.

I was looking forward to meeting this good-looking guy, as well as seeing with my own eyes how those two-people interacted with each other. I scheduled my day off for that special Friday, which couldn't come fast enough.

I felt this pretty girl had me in her grip because of the intriguing stories she had shared with me. Her own family was not even aware of her "job". I had the privilege of being treated closer than family, and that felt somewhat special.

I arrived that Friday around 4 pm, neatly dressed to leave an impression on Enzo. For all I knew, he liked nice things and beautiful woman. I rang the intercom. Marianne just said, "Chantal?" I answered yes, and the door opened immediately. When I got off the elevator, Marianne was already waiting for me with open arms. She hugged me while escorting me inside.

There in the living room stood her handsome man, Enzo. He had black shiny hair and green eyes. No wonder she was in love with him. He was so good looking. He smiled at me and said, "So you are the one Marianne can't stop talking about. You're almost a household name here!" He then hugged me welcome and said, "Chantal, please have a seat. I'm sure you're very familiar around our place by now."

I smiled and said, "Yes, I am."

He proposed a drink, and before I could say anything, Marianne answered for me. "I guess she would like an ice-cold Chardonnay, right Chantal?"

I laughed the way she showed Enzo how familiar she was with what I liked to drink. I said, "Yes, that's excellent; you know it, girl."

Enzo went to the kitchen and came back with two white wine glasses and one red. "Chianti," he said smiling at me. "You guessed it, Chantal. Italians stick to their roots and Italian wine."

We toasted, holding our glasses in the air while Enzo said, "To friendship that's so rare to find." I agreed with his statement. While I sipped my wine, I glanced over to Marianne, who had a bright smile and a little twinkle in her beautiful eyes. I couldn't make anything of it just yet.

While Enzo was busy in the kitchen cooking our wonderful meal (the smell of garlic made me very hungry), Marianne said, "After dinner, when Enzo has left around 6pm, I would like to take you out to a place you haven't been yet, I think.

"We will take my car. It's easier, and we can visit some of my friends on American Boulevard. It's a private club. Is that okay with you, Chantal?"

"Sure," I agreed. "I can't wait to taste Enzo's cooking first and to meet your friends later." I thought this would be a special night. I could feel it.

Marianne didn't need to lift a finger to help Enzo. He set up the dinner table and brought out all the food, which looked delicious – grilled calamari with homemade tartar sauce and ravioli with lobster pieces in a light pink cream sauce. He waved at us to come and taste his handiwork!

He was not only handsome, but a good cook too. He told me while we were devouring this great food that he had a chef's degree, but liked to wait on tables more because of the interaction with customers. He added, "As a chef, you're always stuck in the kitchen, and that's not me." I told him, I totally understood. Being a hostess myself, I liked to interact with people as well. *As a matter of fact,* I thought, *all three of us were somewhat customer oriented, but in different categories, especially beautiful Marianne!*

Enzo did not ask me too many questions about myself. I figured he must have had some feedback from Marianne about me. I didn't mind. I was happy we didn't get into any conversations about my life or anybody else's life. I was very happy I had met Enzo. How lucky this girl was: He was handsome, made good money, and was an excellent cook. On top of all that, he allowed her to do whatever she liked (if she stayed within the boundaries of the agreement they had made with each other.) Who could ask for more?

By the time most of the food had disappeared into our stomachs, he apologized and said, "Sorry ladies, I have to change and leave for work soon. I hope you girls don't mind cleaning up and putting things away?"

We both said at the same time, "No, not at all," although Marianne added the word "honey".

I thanked Enzo for his hospitality, the great food, and the opportunity to have a chat with him. I stood up and hugged him. His body felt muscular and strong. I wanted to hug him a little longer but had to let go. It wouldn't have looked right. I told myself: *He has been taken by my friend for the last 5 years, so stop it!* He rushed to the bedroom to change, came back ten minutes later, and without hesitation kissed his girlfriend passionately the "French way". It didn't bother them that I was standing there and watching the two lovebirds lip-locking in a sexy way.

His hands were gliding over her body, caressing her breasts gently for a few seconds and then slowly lowering his hands to her buttocks, squeezing them. She giggled. It made her sound like a teenager. She told him, "Enough already. I'll see you tonight, sweetheart, okay."

After witnessing this "goodbye-see-you-later show", I rushed quickly into the kitchen, and rinsed the dishes under cold water to cool me off. I stacked them quickly into the dishwasher. Was I feeling a bit jealous and aroused? I had a warm glow inside that came over me, but at the same time, it was wonderful to witness this loving couple.

CHAPTER 6

Marianne rushed to help me with the dishes after I heard the door shut. She apologized and said, "Sorry but Enzo always kisses me like he's never going to see me again!"

I laughed and told her not to worry. "That's what love is all about, isn't it?"

She rolled her eyes. "I guess so," she whispered blushing. "Let's hurry up and get out of here. By the way, did you like the food?"

I quickly answered, "Yes, of course. I'll come over for a dinner made by muscular chef Enzo any time!" I couldn't resist saying the word muscular!

Everything was cleaned up in no time. It seemed as if Marianne was in a hurry to introduce me to her friends. When she came back out of her bedroom ten minutes later, she was dressed to kill. I was stunned at her beauty. Thank goodness, I was well dressed too.

"All right," she said, "let's go to the garage, take my car, and have some fun." Arriving at the lower level of the building, we came to a halt at her white Mustang convertible. Yes, you guessed it; it had red leather seats.

I had only seen that kind of car in the movies. She opened the door to let me slide into the passenger seat and adjusted the seat with the touch of a button.

I looked at her and she quickly said, "Yes, this is my amazing dream car – a fully automatic Mustang V8. I love it."

"Who wouldn't love a car like this?" I told her. I could still smell the distinct "new car smell", especially with the leather seats. Marianne put the car in the "D" position and off we went. I felt like royalty in this one-of-a-kind car that in the 1970s was hardly seen in France. At least I had never seen one before.

We drove about 30 minutes until we reached the American Boulevard. She parked the car close to the club where we were going.

"Destiny Club for woman only" was written on the entrance brick wall. It was one of many enormous houses in a Renaissance style. Three stairs up, we landed in a hallway where Marianne knocked with a brass door knocker attached in the middle of an impressive, huge, double mahogany door.

A muscular bouncer and a robust woman with short hair opened the door and greeted Marianne warmly. Marianne turned towards me and said, "Paula, let me introduce my new friend, Chantal."

The woman looked at me from top to bottom, smiled, and said, "Welcome to the club. Marianne's friends are our friends." She shook my hand firmly.

Paula stepped aside to let us in to the area where all the music and laughter was coming from. As soon as Marianne entered, the owners of the club called out her name and blew kisses towards us. The two women, Denise and Patty, came from behind the bar and hugged Marianne, while Marianne introduced me to both as her new friend. Denise who looked like the decision maker said, "The first drinks are on the house," and asked us what we wanted to drink. I chose a rum and Coke, while Marianne had a brandy.

We both slowly advanced into the crowd, hearing some of the girls calling out to Marianne, "Hello *ma belle* (hi beautiful)." They waved at her while observing me with a question mark on their faces. It made me blush, but I felt proud at the same time to be the friend of a well-known girl in the establishment. It was exciting to flank Marianne inside a club I had never heard of before.

Marianne told me not to worry. "These younger girls are here for the thrill; some of them are real lesbians and have their partner with them, and of course, you and I are here for the fun." She laughed. "I wanted you to get to know my secret club; it's a place where I can be myself with no men around – just lots of nice women."

She then gulped her cognac in one shot and ordered another one, asking me if I wanted another drink. I needed another drink. This place made me thirsty, I told her. We both laughed. It was crowded and warm near the dance floor. We both found a place near the bar and hopped onto barstools, while Marianne ordered our drinks. I looked around, watching all the happy people chatting in a circle, some holding hands.

The dance floor was not that large, but it was packed with couples dancing to a romantic slow song. They were almost glued to each other. I felt kind of comfortable among these lesbian girls. It did not bother me at all, even though it was my first time at this somewhat hidden private club. Suddenly, I felt something ice cold against my arm and saw Marianne holding my rum and Coke against me. She said, "Here to cool off a bit," and we both burst out laughing. Then still smiling, she said, "Are you okay? Do you like it here, or should we go elsewhere?"

I looked at her amused, and said, "Do you see me grumpy or hiding somewhere? To answer you: Yes, I feel good here and will come back with you anytime you want to go to this place.

Marianne nodded her head and said, "We'll come as often as you like. I will make you a member of the club, so that way you can come by yourself if I'm not available, when you feel like it, deal?" *By myself*, I thought, *I don't think that will happen. I'm a straight girl, and I like men. Why would I come here alone?* But I agreed to become a member and thanked her for the offer.

While we were consuming our second drink, Marianne's attention went to the back of the club to a fair-skinned, gorgeous girl with short, black hair. Her eyes looked almost as dark as her hair. She stared back at her.

I could see a twinkle in Marianne's blue eyes. I noticed she knew the woman, and I asked her who the girl in the back was. Marianne told me her name was Rita. "She's here every weekend or at least every time I am here. I think she has had a crush on me for the longest time; I can feel it. Rita has asked me a few times to dance with her, and the way she holds me, I can feel the warmth of her body against mine. It's as if she wants to crawl inside of me, you know what I mean, Chantal?" *I could imagine it, for sure.* She added, "I think she's even a few years younger than me, but who cares right?"

CHAPTER 7

Marianne continued saying, "Rita has repeatedly asked me for a dinner date, which I always refuse, with a good excuse, of course. I pretend I'm interested in her. It makes me feel good, and it keeps the adrenaline rush flowing for both of us when we meet. Maybe one day I will accept her invitation and go for dinner with her. But I'm not ready yet. I feel fine just pretending for now!

I was stunned to hear her say that. She had a hard-working, good-looking boyfriend. Why on earth would she go on an adventure with Rita? Just for fun? And in what way did Rita like Marianne – only to check her out or to go to bed with her? Did she know she had a good bank account? And why was Marianne interested in Rita?

This became insanely interesting to me. *What would follow next,* I thought. I hadn't seen anything yet. Just as I was absorbing everything around me, Rita made her way towards us. She held out her arms and embraced Marianne and kissed her on both cheeks. Looking at me sideways, she asked Marianne who I was. She said, "Rita, this is Chantal, my new friend, for more than a month now." She added, "She is not lesbian, so don't get any ideas in your head." We all laughed. I rolled my eyes at Marianne and blushed.

"This place is new to Chantal, and I wanted her to know where I hang out sometimes." She smiled and winked at me. Swiftly Rita hugged me and for a few seconds, I thought, *how pleasant it is being hugged by a lesbian woman.* It did not feel any different than getting a hug from my cousin. She made it feel like she knew me. I liked her instantly.

Deep down, I felt something would happen between the two of them. It was written in their eyes. We started a conversation between the three of us. Rita wanted to know a few things about me like what I did for a living and where I was from. I assumed she already knew about Marianne's job, as we didn't mention anything about Marianne's work. Rita was only interested in me. The music changed, and Rita invited Marianne for a slow dance. I knew for sure that this was going to happen eventually. Since Rita only saw Marianne occasionally on a weekend, she didn't waste any time. Marianne smiled at me and said mockingly, "See you soon." She got off her bar stool, slipped her hand into Rita's, and headed to the crowded dance floor. As I watched them, I felt a warm glow and thought how mesmerizing this all was. All this love around me was so serene.

Suddenly someone tapped on my shoulder I looked behind me and saw a young, 19 or 20-year-old, pretty tom boy girl smiling at me, asking me to dance with her. I almost fell off my bar stool, blushed, and hesitated for a second. Then reality kicked in. I was at a lesbian private club. This was a normal thing, so why not? I shook my head and said, "Yes, of course."

She took my hand and introduced herself, "Hi, I'm Diane." I told her my name and hit the dance floor for a slow dance. It looked like this was the best and only way to get connected. Diane was very outgoing and pleasant; she took the "lead" as a man would. To my surprise, she was an excellent dance partner. She had a firm grip around my waist, without being overly possessive.

My eyes were searching for Marianne somewhere on the dance floor. When I locked eyes with her, we both rolled our eyes, but in a good way. She gave me the thumps up while winking without any of our partners noticing it.

This was amazing. I would have never in my wildest dreams thought I would ever dance with a woman, or in this case, a young girl. This was a new world for me. I figured Marianne had more in store for me. I couldn't wait for the next surprise. We all came back from the dance floor at the same time. Diane walked away and thanked me for the dance. Rita and Marianne strolled towards the bar, chatting away about who knows what. We ordered another drink for all of us. It looked as if we were not going home for awhile.

By now the club was overcrowded, and everyone was glued to each other like canned sardines. I felt suffocated, twisting and turning my body against all these strangers, all women who didn't seem to mind… Marianne saw me getting a bit uncomfortable and asked if I would like to go somewhere else. I shook my head and said, "Yes, that's a good idea," while Rita quickly asked if she could come along.

Marianne agreed, and we wrestled ourselves to the exit. The cool air was refreshing when we walked out the door. The idea was to go to the nightclub, where Marianne and I had met for the first time. Since Rita didn't mind mingling with both men and woman, she tagged along.

Rita took her car while I took a seat in Marianne's Mustang. On the way to the Blue Note Disco, she giggled nonstop, saying how funny this was and how happy she was that I was enjoying it. Rita followed us to the Blue Note, where we spent the rest of the night, till 2 am, dancing and chatting the night away. Rita went home, and so did we. On the way home, Marianne asked me, if I had a good time. I answered, "Of course, this was a pleasant surprise, and I wouldn't mind going there again with you some time soon."

She smiled and said, "Glad you liked it." We arrived at the underground parking in her building. She dropped me near my car before driving inside and said, "Chantal, thank you for the wonderful evening, and keep this outing to yourself, okay!" Again, Enzo was not aware of her visits to the "woman's only private club". I told her she could count on me and not to worry. We hugged each other and promised to call each other in a couple of days.

CHAPTER 8

When I drove home, I had a re-run of that evening in my head, and I wondered how it would end between Marianne and Rita. I could sense there was a mutual, undeniable attraction between both of them. Rita seemed smitten with Marianne, more so than Marianne was with her. If this was again a game for Marianne, I knew this was not a game for Rita. She was madly in love with her; it was written all over her. I thought: *You better watch out, Marianne. This could become either beautiful or ugly.*

A few weeks later, Marianne called me and said, "Are you free this Saturday, Chantal?"

I said, "Yes, I am, Marianne. Why? Are we having Enzo's Italian food again?"

She laughed and said, "No, but I would like to take you out to have a bite to eat, and after dinner, I would like to go to 'our' private club, if that's okay with you?" I agreed. We would meet up at the Italian restaurant she had in mind. I loved Italian food, so I did not hesitate to accept the invitation.

We arrived around 7 pm at the restaurant called Trattoria Roma. It had a nice interior with a typically Italian style, and the food was excellent. It seemed Marianne was well known there. Tony, the owner, came to our table and greeted us; he kissed Marianne on both cheeks. Then he looked at me with a twinkle in his eyes, took my hand, and softly planted his moist lips on the upper part of my fingers. Oh my… was it because I was blonde and blue-eyed? He could see I wasn't from an Italian family. I was flattered. Italian men are known to be charming; they knew how to make a woman feel special.

After our meal, I asked Marianne, "So what's the urgency for going to the Destiny Club? We were just there a little while ago?" She said she just wanted to go there and didn't know why. I could see she wasn't telling me everything. I knew she wanted to see Rita again. I would have made a bet on it, but I didn't have anyone to bet with! I agreed with her. I didn't mind going there. I wanted to find out if my gut feeling was telling me the truth.

She paid the bill and left a huge tip for the waiter, who hugged her since they all knew her and Enzo. Then the waiter reached for my hand. His lips elegantly touched my fingers. He looked and smiled at me with his blue-green eyes. It felt very pleasant and gave me a warm feeling. I turned red in the face. He was so good looking. I would say "yes" in a heartbeat if he would ask me out. Thank goodness, we quickly walked out to the car and drove off to "our" club; we had nicknamed it "our" club, so no one would hear the name Destiny.

We arrived at the club, parked the car, and entered through the massive front door. I was in love with it, probably because it had this special design from another era. Paula opened the door, and smiled at both of us. She had a very masculine build. I would not want to have a fight with her. Suddenly, I had the giggles thinking about rolling on the floor with Paula, trying to have the upper hand…hilarious.

As soon as the owners of the club saw Marianne, they again both welcomed us like we were family members. How wonderful it was to be welcomed by strangers who treated you as family. Never had I seen this in any other private club – not even at the "Blue Note", where if you were a repeat customer, they said hello and that was it.

Right away Marianne's eyes were looking for Rita, but we didn't see her. We ordered a drink and sat at the bar as usual, watching all the girls and women talking, dancing, and hugging each other. This was now all familiar to me. I felt very comfortable as a "regular" girl.

Marianne asked me if I was okay with spending the night there and not going to the other club later. I nodded. Of course, I'm okay with that. If I'm with you, and we have fun, I'm not going anywhere."

She smiled, and out of the blue, she said, "I came here because I wanted to see Rita tonight."

I looked at her and said, "I knew it from the moment you asked me to spend the evening here."

She started laughing, throwing her hair from left to right, and grabbed my hand saying, "You, Chantal, are a mind reader. I give you that." We both started laughing out loud, hugging each other while sitting on our bar stools. All the girls around us were laughing together with us, not knowing why we were giggling so hard. We were just amused with what Marianne had said – *I was a mind reader*.

Suddenly Marianne felt some soft lips against her cheek, it was Rita. She had come in while we were both in this laughing mode.

Marianne turned around and locked eyes with her. They hugged and kissed. Rita then looked at me and said, "Hi Chantal, nice to see you again," and hugged me as well. I knew something was in the air. It was almost palpable. It wasn't long after Rita ordered her drink that she asked Marianne to dance with her, which Marianne happily accepted. I watched them dancing cheek to cheek. Love was in the air. It felt tender, beautiful, and there was nothing wrong with the picture. These two people were in love and were not afraid to show it.

Why did Marianne tell me she was "only pretending" with Rita? This slow dance showed otherwise. She held Rita tight against her body. She just wanted to keep it a secret for now, but I knew there was more than that in the making in the way Marianne behaved.

When the music changed to Bob Marley's reggae or Elvis Presley's rock and roll, they both left the dance floor and walked back to the bar, holding hands.

We talked about everything that was going on in our lives, and some friends came over who wanted to say hi to Rita and Marianne and get to know me as well. Marianne and Rita were almost never in their seats. They danced the night away. I saw them kissing and not just on the cheek. It made we weak, but happy to see them holding each other as if there was no tomorrow. The scene was seductive and hot.

I went to the bathroom, when it was a slow dance to avoid having to dance with anyone, only because I could see and feel it would not be that difficult to fall in love with some of the woman or girls, even though I was a "straight girl". I just didn't think I was ready for this. *Not tonight anyway.*

CHAPTER 9

By the end of the night, around 1 pm, Marianne asked me if I would mind if she and Rita went to another lesbian club called Cinq Anno. If I wanted, I could join them. I said, "No, that's all right. You go ahead, you little love birds. I'll go to the Blue Note instead." They both smiled, hugged me, waved goodbye to the owners, and took off. By now, everyone who knew Rita and Marianne had seen them both taking off to another place for the first time and wondered, just like me, where they were heading.

When I went to pay for my drinks, Pat told me everything had been taken care of by Marianne. I thought: *Sweet Marianne, such a loving, giving girl. But what's going to happen from here on? What about Enzo?*

The next day Sunday, I could not stop myself and called Marianne in the afternoon. I usually would never call her on a Sunday, as I knew Enzo would be there. But I couldn't resist the idea. I wanted to know what she had done or where she had gone the previous night when she left with Rita.

Marianne picked up the phone. I said, "Hey girl, it's me, Chantal."

She answered, "Wait a minute, I have to go to the bathroom to talk." I heard her walking quickly to one of the bathrooms that had a phone installed on the wall, probably far away from Enzo's ears. She said, "Hey Chantal, how are you? Did you end up at the Blue Note?"

I said, "Of course, I danced the rest of the night away with some good-looking guys. And what about you and Rita, where did you go?"

Now she started whispering. She said, "We did go to the Cinq Anno, had some more drinks, and made out on the couch at the bar. By the time she escorted me to my car an hour later, we were on top of each other in the back seat. I never had this kind of chemistry with anyone before, not even with Enzo. Oh my, Chantal, I never felt this way ever. Her lips were everywhere. I just wasn't expecting this overwhelming feeling. Just thinking about how much I enjoyed that night is enough to accept another date with Rita. I think…no wait, I *feel* I'm in love! Is that possible?"

"I don't want to have this feeling, but it's here."

I was silent for a few seconds, swallowed, and then said, "Marianne, let's not get carried away. Maybe you were both drunk, didn't think clearly, and your female hormones got the best of you both."

She said, still whispering, "No, Chantal, I don't think so. I agreed to go for dinner with her this coming Thursday. She has asked me this for the longest time now, and I can no longer resist. I want to get to know her better."

I had tears welling up in my eyes. *What was she doing? What was she feeling for this woman? What was going to happen if Enzo found out? And her family?* I was afraid about what could happen to Marianne at this point. I said, "Well, Marianne, if that's what you want, go for it. Find out what it is you feel for this woman, and what Rita's feelings are for you."

She answered, "Thank you, Chantal, for understanding. You are the only one I can rely on and who knows my deepest secrets. I love you like a sister. Thank you, sweetie. I will keep you posted after my date with Rita this Thursday. Maybe we can get together at your place for a change? How about it?"

I said, "Yes, that's an idea. Call me Friday, and let's meet when we both aren't working, all right?"

We hung up the phone. My mind was racing wildly, and I wondered how in the world this whole thing between Rita and Marianne would end. I didn't think it would end well. However, I could tell by the way Marianne was all bubbly and ready to see Rita this Thursday that I could be very wrong. The next day, I went to work, my mind still wondering what would happen if Enzo found out. I hoped it would not get out of hand between the two of them. I knew he loved Marianne deeply and was not about to let go of her to any man, let alone a woman!

Thursday came and went. I was all excited to hear from Marianne. She called me at work around 5 pm and said Enzo was going to work. She asked if she could come to my place and see me after I was done working at 5:30 pm. I agreed.

I already had some food in the fridge from the day before. I knew she would come to my apartment and wanted to pamper her like she always did to me I gave her the address and waited somewhat restlessly until she arrived at 5:45 pm.

I opened the door as soon as she rang the intercom doorbell. We hugged, and I showed her the way to my apartment and living room, which were tiny compared to hers. She threw herself into my love seat, with her legs curled beneath her. I knew then she had a story to tell and wasn't going anywhere soon. I offered her a drink and sat close to her, so she could lean or cry on my shoulders if she needed to.

CHAPTER 10

"Chantal," she said, "I had the most unbelievable night ever."

I said, "Then let's hear about it."

She took a long breath and smiled. "Well, when I met Rita at the restaurant, we had a nice dinner and some wine. The way Rita looked at me made me melt. Her fingers moved through mine while we were at the table, squeezing them softly. I got all warm inside and wanted to kiss her right there and then. Good thing the restaurant was packed, so we both had to hold our feelings at bay." We both laughed when she said that.

"When we were done with our dinner, she asked me if I wanted to see where she lived and go for a nightcap. You can imagine, Chantal, I said, 'yes of course.'"

I thought: *For sure, Rita had something else in mind than a nightcap.*

I sipped at my wine and said, "What did you think when you accepted her invitation. Was the adrenaline flowing when you drove to her house?"

"Yes, it did. My body was shaking with desire to be with her. Never before had I felt this way; the thought of being alone with Rita was ridiculously exciting. When we reached her house, she opened the car door to let me out, and kissed me passionately, pushing me against the car. The sound of our breathing was swallowed by each other. I groaned, feeling her body against mine. Remember, we were outside, in front of her house, surrounded by the stars and the moonlight. I couldn't believe it; she bedazzled me."

Marianne continued, saying, "I knew Rita had wanted me for the longest time ever, and she did not waste any time showing it. She opened the front door of her house, and we both stumbled inside. The passion now had the upper hand. Rita softly said, 'The couch or upstairs to my bedroom?'

"It was all fuzzy in my head. I could not think clearly. All I wanted was to be in her arms. I answered, 'Whatever you want.' She guided me upstairs. Once we were in her bedroom, she took me by the waist and threw me softly onto the bed. I quickly kicked off my shoes.

"Rita whispered, 'Oh Marianne, you're so beautiful.' She started to undress me slowly. When my bra came off, she caressed my breasts, as if they were made from silk."

A thought flashed through my head as Marianne said this. I knew they were not that soft since I had the privilege of touching them a few months previously.

Marianne continued. "Her tongue met my nipples and licked and sucked them as if they were ice cream. I was so aroused; you have no idea. She lowered her head towards my stomach, kissing every inch she came across. I was holding my breath, moaning like a schoolgirl, and twisting and curling my body like a snake, as she slipped off my silk panties. She separated my legs gently and her hand moved down, skimming my waist, until she reached my clitoris. She caressed it gently in a circular way. All the while, I was moaning and thinking, *Holy fuck, this is extremely erotic.*

"She then put one of her fingers softly inside me, stroking and caressing me all over my body with the other hand roaming freely, anywhere she wanted. Slowly she dropped on her knees. I could see her in front of me, her lips still kissing me, lower and lower towards my belly button and to where her finger had been before. Her tongue glided onto my clitoris and moved back and forth, up and down. We are both breathing heavily at that point. Holy shit…Chantal, let me tell you I was so hot, it took my breath away.

"That was the ultimate climax for me. I was now wild with excitement as a sensation rippled through my entire body. I don't know how many times I had an orgasm, but lots. The pleasure was indescribable. There are no words for it. It did not take long. We were both kissing each other all over our bodies, rolling around in the bed. It felt like an earthquake. Her tongue wrestled inside my mouth, as if she was trying to find any cavity…"

At that, we both burst out laughing. But at the same time, I thought: *Wow, this was anything but dull.*

"Chantal, sorry to say it, but I think I'm in love."

There she said it again. I said, "What about Enzo?"

She shook her head. "I know it's going to be difficult to hide it. I'll try and see how long my excitement for Rita will last and hers for me. As it stands now, I can't wait to see her again and not at our private club, if you know what I mean. I want to be alone with her."

"Of course," I said, "I know."

As I poured another drink in my glass, Marianne gave me her empty glass and jokingly said, "Please fill this one up too." We both took another sip of our wine, as Marianne let out a sigh of relief and said, "Chantal, I don't know how long this will go on, but as long as Enzo doesn't know or find out, promise me you won't tell a soul, right?"

"Not a peep, Marianne. That's a promise." *Again, I had to promise another secret*! I went to the kitchen and brought out some cold cuts, cheese, and crispy French bread. I needed a break and to talk about something other than her "exciting hot encounter" with Rita, which made me feel like I wanted sex right at that moment!

However, while munching on our food, she could not stop talking about Rita and how gentle she was. She knew for sure Rita had been deeply in love with her for the longest time, but hadn't had the chance before to persuade Marianne to go out for dinner and a nightcap at her house. Rita was an accountant for a huge financial firm and made good money. Marianne had told her what kind of business she was in and that she only did it for the money.

Rita was somewhat shocked to hear that her beautiful Marianne had been having sex with men as a "job" for the last two years. And she was even more stunned to hear that Enzo was okay with it!

I said, "That is not unusual for someone who had a regular job to be stunned about what you're doing for a living. Not everyone could do or agree with what you are doing, Marianne. I know the money is the main reason, but there's got to be a way to do something else later in life. You're not going to stay twenty something forever."

Marianne shook her head, and said, "Yes, I know. Someday I will have to choose between money and a normal life and job. I'm slowly getting enough of men all together. Why do you think I accepted Rita's invitation! I get the goose bumps some days when customers touch me when I'm at Topaz.

"I'm also fed up listening to their stupid stories. So, I see your point about it being time for a job change. I'm so glad I can talk to you, Chantal." We hugged for a few seconds. I knew she needed someone to confide in, especially after her date with Rita. I knew she was in a serious struggle between her job, Rita, and her boyfriend. I could not give her advice on either one of them. Marianne would do what her heart would tell her to do, as simple as that.

CHAPTER 11

A few weeks went by when I had a call from Marianne on a Wednesday. She asked me to come and see her that night if I wasn't working.

I was off that day and went over to her place around six. She let me in, and I could see she had been crying. She hugged me, and we took a seat next to each other. I asked her, "What's wrong? You look unhappy for the first time since I've known you."

She then started telling me how she was in a dilemma. She was thinking of moving in with Rita, but was not sure yet if that was a good idea because she was afraid of how Enzo would react to this. I told her that I thought it was too soon to tell if things between her and Rita were solid enough to make the move.

She looked at me and said, "See Chantal, that's why I wanted you over here. You make me see things more clearly. My heart wants to, but my mind is still wondering if it is the right decision. I don't know anymore. I think about Rita day and night. I want her. I feel her touching me even though she isn't here.

"I can't get her out of my mind." She went to the kitchen and brought us a glass of wine; we needed it. Marianne was still looking at me with a question mark on her beautiful face, almost begging me in silence to give her an answer, which I was not about to do. I was her friend, and she could rely on me any time for whatever she needed. But it was out of the question for me to give her advice about breaking up with Enzo for Rita; that wasn't for me to say.

I stayed with her till around 10 pm, talking mostly about Rita. She also said that a distance had developed between Enzo and her, and she thought he could feel something was up. If he knew that Marianne was in love with a woman, it would not end well. When I left her place, I felt danger lurking. I didn't know when it would strike or where, but it was imminent. I told her to be careful.

I got a call Sunday morning around 9 am. It was Marianne in tears. She told me she had invited Rita to her apartment instead of going to Rita's house on Saturday night since Enzo was away working, and he never got home until 1 or 2 in the morning.

Marianne wanted Rita to see where she lived. They had a few drinks and made love in Marianne and Enzo's bedroom. Marianne said, "The sensation and the passion between us lasted so long and was so intense I never wanted her to leave me. She knows exactly the right places on my body to send me to the moon and back." She sighed.

"Afterwards, we were both exhausted and a bit tipsy. We fell asleep in each other's arms. That's when Enzo came home a few hours later but still earlier than expected. He found us both in bed. He started yelling at us. I think the floor below us heard it all. He told me I was a slut, while Rita got up quickly and got dressed. Enzo pushed Rita against the wall, put his fist against her cheek, and told her he was coming after her if he ever saw her in our apartment or with his girl again."

While she was telling me this, I had goose bumps and had to swallow a few times. Marianne continued, "He threw Rita out the door and locked it. He was furious as he came back in the bedroom. He slapped me a few times in the face, apologizing at the same time for slapping me, which he has never done before.

"I know, Chantal, maybe you think Enzo never would have thought he would catch me in his own bed with a woman, right?"

I said, "Yes, that's right." I could somehow imagine how he must have felt.

"He asked me how long this had been going on. I said it had been a few weeks and told him right there and then, I was in love with Rita. He fell on his knees and begged me to let go of Rita. He said it was just a fling and I wasn't a real lesbian; I was just exploring new things. He said he was ready to forgive me. In a way, I felt sorry that he had witnessed me in bed with Rita, but on the other hand, I was relieved. I now had to decide which way to go, and no more hiding."

" What did you say to him at that moment?" I asked.

Marianne answered, "I told him I was hooked and wanted to live with Rita. I said I still loved him, but I was somehow disgusted with men touching me. I only wanted to be touched by Rita."

I thought: *At that moment, Enzo realized he had lost his gorgeous Marianne to a woman.*

Marianne continued. "He told me he would kill both of us if I left him. The moment he said the word 'kill', he made me scared. I fled to the bathroom – the one with a phone – and called the police. I filed a complaint against him. I repeated his words that he wanted to kill me and my friend Rita if I moved out and left him.

"The police asked me to get some of my clothing together, so I could leave the apartment as soon as they arrived. They were on their way and asked me to wait for them. It made me feel safer knowing the police would be there soon. They arrived 10 minutes later. While I packed a few things, they said if I needed other belongings I could call them, and they would escort me safely out with whatever items were mine. So I took a small suitcase while the police were watching and left escorted by them. Enzo kept staring at me in disbelief. The police gave Enzo a warning not to go after me at that time because if the incident escalated, jail was waiting for him.

CHAPTER 12

"Oh Marianne, what a nightmare! Where did you go?"

"I am at my mom's house now. I told her Enzo and I had an argument, and I needed to stay at her house for a few days. She could see it was serious and told me I could stay as long as needed. I was afraid to go to Rita's house because I didn't know if Enzo would follow me or not. To tell you the truth, I fear for my life and Rita's.

"You know, Chantal, I think I became disgusted not with Enzo really, but with men altogether because of the 'work' I do. As soon as I got intimate with Rita, I knew men were not important anymore. Being with Rita was a new world that opened up and a sweet one; do you understand what I'm saying?"

I said, "Of course, I do. I'm just as scared as you are right now for what's coming in the next few days and weeks."

Poor Enzo, I thought. *Being a young, handsome Italian and catching your girlfriend in bed with a female would be hard to swallow. It would be for any man, let alone a proud Italian.*

"What are you going to do from here on I asked her? Are you going to work or taking a week off?"

"Yes," she said, "I called Gina and told her I have big issues to deal with and will not be available until further notice. Don't forget, my family does not know anything about the work I do. I only hope Enzo won't tell them out of revenge.

"That would be a disaster for the whole family, especially my mom. I would lose all her trust, and I don't want that to happen. I love her too much. I will tell her in my own time. I will stay here for at least a week, and then I will meet Rita to see what we are going to do and if she is willing to let me move in with her. I'll keep you posted about the situation, okay Chantal?"

"Okay, sweetie," I said, "just be careful wherever you hang out from now on."

I almost had a nervous breakdown after hearing all that. I was happy to have Marianne as my best friend, but now I became like a worried sister over the situation she was in. *How I could help her? Should I speak with Rita? Should I call Enzo? Neither one of them would be the right thing to do.* I decided to wait till Marianne spoke to Rita and see what happened from there on. I needed a drink when I came home. I watched a bit of TV and tried to catch some sleep, but that was more difficult than I anticipated.

The next morning, while getting myself ready to go to work at noon, I couldn't stop thinking about poor Enzo. Did he deserve that? Was the love affair over for him and his beautiful Marianne? How angry or sad he must feel right at this moment. All these questions, but I had no answers for them. I had to wait till Marianne called me.

It was Wednesday evening; I got a call from Marianne. She said she had moved out with police escort and took everything she needed and that belonged to her. She said, "I left most of the furniture to Enzo. Rita was in heaven and immediately told me I could come and live with her as soon as I wanted, which of course I did. There was no way, Chantal, I could have another normal relationship with Enzo. Besides he would never trust me again, so I made the decision very quickly when Rita said I could move in.

"It feels weird living with a woman. A woman who makes me happy though, but still I'm not used to it yet. It's too soon, I guess. I'll tell my mother someday what happened and why, but I have to find another job first."

I said, "Well yes, another job should be your priority, wouldn't you agree?"

She laughed and said, "I knew you were going to say that. But for now, I am going to take some time off my old job and not resign just yet.

"Rita and I are going on a vacation in the Alps to do some skiing. There's lots of snow by now in that region, and after that, we'll get a massage from a professional massage therapist. We will have lots of good food, drinks, and relaxing. We both need it. I'm tired. It all came so fast and unexpectedly. I need a break."

I agreed 100% with Marianne. I asked her when they would leave.

She said, "This coming weekend, December 12, for eight days. I'll call you when we are back and maybe you can come by and have dinner with us. I would love to see you and tell you all about our trip and everything else for that matter."

I replied, "For sure, just let me know and I'll be there."

CHAPTER 13

The week Marianne was away on her ski trip with Rita, I got a call from Enzo. I almost dropped the receiver, I immediately recognized his voice and said, "Hi Enzo, what can I do for you?"

In a soft voice, he said, "Hi Chantal. I just wanted someone to talk to, who knows the story about Marianne and me and the woman she's with."

I had to sit down, but I asked him how I could help.

He said, "How did that came about? How did she meet this lesbian woman? Didn't the two of you met at the Blue Note disco?"

I said, "Yes, we did." I wasn't sure I should tell him about the private club Destiny, so I told him a little white lie and said some girls invited us to a club for "women only" one Saturday night. We didn't know it was a private club. We found out once we got there, but didn't think anything of it and wanted to explore how it was different from a "normal" disco.

Enzo didn't interrupt me. I could hear him breathing and felt somewhat sorry for him and that he had been lied to after everything he went through during his 5 years together with Marianne, whom he trusted and loved. He was such a handsome guy and a good cook too. I'd give anything to meet a guy like him.

He said, "Is it there that she met this woman Rita?"

"Yes, Enzo. I was there with her on another occasion weeks later. We were bored at the Blue Note, so we took off to that private club where only woman are allowed. You have to be a member and introduced by a member.

"Marianne and I became members through Rita. I never knew Rita had a crush on Marianne the first time she saw her. But Marianne told me she knew and could feel Rita had a crush on her. She didn't want to give in, so she just pretended and had fun with Rita. It was like a game for Marianne or so I thought.

"Enzo, my friend," I said, "do you need to know more? I don't have much more to tell you about them at this time. I have not seen Marianne or Rita in a while. What I just told you about how they met is what you needed to know. Will that close the chapter for you?"

He took a few seconds to answer me, and then said, "Yes, it's okay, Chantal. I have heard enough. I only needed to know how long this was going on behind my back – whether it was one year or two, but it seems like this is very new for Marianne. I hope she will be happy in the future with this woman because I can not take her back as much as I love and miss her. It will take a long time to get over it, but this is the end for us. "As a man, you can only take so much." I silently agreed with his statement.

"I want to thank you, Chantal, for telling me all this because I know you are very close to Marianne, and hopefully your friendship with her will be forever. Please keep an eye out for her because she hasn't known this woman long enough, and sex alone won't make a relationship last. There's more to a relationship than sex."

I thought: *Yes, Enzo, you're so right.*

I promised Enzo I would do just that. I told him I considered Marianne like a sister I never had and would watch over her if she allowed me to be her friend. I felt sorry for Enzo. *What a shame. He is such a good man and has lost the love of his life. How will he ever explain to his parents and family in Italy why Marianne and he broke up after 5 years? I don't think he will say a woman came into Marianne's life!*

CHAPTER 14

The week went by fast, and Marianne called me as soon as they were back from their trip. She asked me if I would come over to their house for dinner on Sunday night. I for sure would; I wanted to see where Rita's house was and her way of living. Marianne gave me the address and time – Sunday evening at 5 pm. I rang the doorbell at Rita's house. It seemed to be a nice house, and I hoped Marianne was happy here. Rita opened the door and gave me a big hug. Marianne was right behind her and grabbed a hold of me, kissing me on both cheeks. She held me close to her as if she hadn't seen me in years. It felt good. She knew she could trust me like no other.

The interior of the house felt warm and inviting. Rita guided me to the living room where I sank into one of the couches. A bottle of champagne was waiting for us, resting deep in an ice bucket, waiting to be uncorked. At almost the same time, they said, "Welcome to our house. We'll have a toast to you, Chantal, our best friend, and to a new beginning of our lives together."

I felt honoured when they said that. I was happy for Marianne and Rita. Only time would tell if they were meant for each other and if they would spend their lives together from here on. Marianne took the initiative to fill our champagne glasses all the way up to the rim, as she always did when pouring wine. All three of us sipped the cooled, expensive Moet & Chandon champagne and said "cheers". I added, "To a good life and anything that will come after, wishing you both all the best there is to life."

"So tell me about you trip, I said. "How was it?" They both started to tell me about what a wonderful time they had and how relaxing it was. Then Rita excused herself to go to the kitchen where she was preparing homemade French fries with a porter house steak and béarnaise sauce, my favourite.

Suddenly Marianne jumped of her sofa and took a seat next to me on the couch. She needed to tell me about the time she and Rita had while at the resort. Now whispering, she said, "Chantal, I don't think I knew what love/sex was until I met Rita. I always thought sex is just sex, nothing more, but I was a fool to think that way. I've had to adapt to a whole different kind of love, the love of a woman. The touch of a woman, the scent of a woman is so different than that of a man; it's softer and sweeter. Rita knows how to send me to cloud 9 and back without being rough or macho like most men are. Do you follow me, Chantal?"

I nodded yes without saying a word. Marianne continued, "At the hotel, we had sex in the shower and on the bedroom floor. She stroked my clitoris in the elevator, pushing aside my panties, and putting two of her fingers inside of me to feel how wet I was. I was steamy hot all the while as she caressed my breasts on top of my clothing and her fingers did the work down below…till I had an orgasm, my body shivering. It drove me almost insane in the elevator. Luckily for us, the elevator didn't stop anywhere but at our floor." We both burst out laughing.

"We had sex on the couch in a sweet and tender way. I was mesmerized by how wonderful this was. I think I'll never go back to a man again. I love that woman. The only way to get out of the job I'm doing is to find something else that I like and make decent money, but I have no idea yet where to look."

Rita came out of the kitchen and called both of us to the table, as dinner was ready. It smelled good. Marianne and I grabbed our champagne glasses and headed to our seats in the dining room.

The porter house steak was tender and delicious, and so were the crispy homemade French fries. Rita and Marianne were seated next to each other; I was at the other end of the table and could see the tender moments between the two lovebirds. We talked and laughed while Rita told her side of the story at the resort and about the fun they had as they got to know each other better. Marianne looked at me smiling. I couldn't help it, but I had the giggles inside, knowing what Marianne had just told me about their sex sending her to cloud 9. I wished I could have been a fly in their room or in the elevator. It was crazy hot with those two.

The after-dinner nightcap was a cognac café latte. I must say, Rita had all the gadgets in the kitchen to make a wonderful dinner and other specialties. She knew how to entertain; I had to give her that.

We wrapped it up around 11 pm; I had to work the next day, but promised to go out with them the following weekend. We promised that after we spent Christmas with family (Marianne with Rita's family and I with my mom and stepdad), we would celebrate as close friends on New Year's Eve. It would be just the three of us, welcoming 1973 in as a New Year and a new beginning for everyone.

They escorted me to the door, hugged me, and said, "We'll have to do this more often, okay Chantal?"

"For sure, we will," I said, and hopped into my car and waved goodbye to them. I never had the chance to tell Marianne that her now ex-boyfriend had called me to find out more about their relationship and how Marianne had met Rita. Maybe it was better not to tell her, since she didn't ask about Enzo or talk about him at all. I thought I would not say anything unless she started a conversation about Enzo.

CHAPTER 15

The following Saturday, Marianne called me to find out if I wanted to come with them to "our" club. I agreed to meet them there at around 8 pm. I had no choice. I knew from now on Marianne only wanted to go dancing and have a good time at the Destiny Club because that's where she and Rita felt they belonged. When I arrived, Paula at the door let me in right away and greeted me, as she knew me by now. I smiled at her and quickly entered the club. Rita and Marianne where sitting at the bar as always. I did not have to look far to find them. We hugged and kissed each other. The owner asked me what I wanted to drink; I ordered a gin and tonic on ice. I needed a large drink. It was hot in there. All the hot young ladies full of adrenaline and hopes of finding a partner made me sweat.

From now on, Rita and Marianne were known as a pair; everyone seemed happy for the couple. They did not hide that they were madly in love. When on the dance floor, they kissed and hugged each other. They were almost glued to each other's body, like they were dancing on "one stone" as the saying goes.

I wondered if this was for real or short term. After a while, I told them I was going to the Blue Note and would talk to them sometime in the week. Marianne was a bit sad to see me go, but understood I was only there because they asked me to come. She did appreciate my effort to come to the club, and made me promise to call her during the week.

On Thursday, I called Marianne as promised at around 4 pm. She picked up the phone and sounded sad and not like herself. I asked her what was wrong. She said she had her first fight with Rita about the job she had. "I told her I was doing it only for the money, and it would take time for me to find something else."

"So, what did Rita say?" I asked.

"She wants me to stop working at the mansion," said Marianne. "She's jealous and doesn't want anyone to touch her 'property'. But Chantal, I am not letting her rule over me like that, you understand that, right?"

"Of course, so what's your plan?"

"Well, I am going back to work next week for a few hours. I will let Rita know that she has nothing to fear about losing me. Men mean nothing to me anymore. She should know that by now and accept my decision."

I said, "Well, I agree that she should not interfere with what you are doing. You will find out soon enough if Rita will allow it and accept it until you find something else."

"Chantal," she said, "I am so glad you understand where I'm coming from. You're the only person in my life right now I can trust enough to say whatever is on my mind. And I get such wise advice from you. Please don't hesitate to call me when you feel like it, okay! If I need you, I will call you, or maybe we could go for coffee sometime, when Rita is working, all right?"

"Sure, Marianne, we will do this soon."

I went home that weekend as I hadn't seen my mom in a while and craved her cooking. She was happy to see me and had made my favourite dish – Belgian endive au gratin with lots of cheese slightly browned under the grill. My mom was the best cook in town. I loved her so much. She wanted to know every detail of what was going on in my life.

So, we chatted until late in the afternoon, but the name "Marianne" was not mentioned in my conversation. Around 4:30 pm, it was time for fresh croissants with jam or cheese and coffee with whipped cream on top. I was in heaven. She reminded me not to forget Christmas Eve dinner and to be there on time. "Don't worry, Mom I won't be late," I said and hugged and kissed her. I drove home around 8 pm, but I was looking forward to coming back. It was good to have a home to go back to and to have a mother who always welcomed me with open arms.

While I drove home, I decided to stop by the club as it was Saturday night and Rita and Marianne were probably at the club too. When I got there 30 minutes later, I stepped into the area where I usually would find Rita and Marianne, but one of the owners told me that the two of them had a fight when they were at the club on Friday night. They had both been banned and could not come back until they stopped fighting and yelling at each other.

This must have been a difficult decision for the club owners since Marianne and Rita were known as big spenders. I was in shock and ordered a drink, thinking I would have to call Marianne and see what was going on. But I would do this on Monday and let the weekend go by. Who knows what was going on between them at this given moment? I was somewhat afraid for Marianne's well being.

CHAPTER 16

On Monday afternoon, I called Marianne at Rita's place; she picked up the phone and right away said, "I'm so relieved you've called, Chantal." I told her what the owners of the club had told me about her and Rita, and that I was worried. She said, "Rita is overly jealous and now has the idea that one of the owners – Patty to be precise – has a crush on me because she pampers me a bit too much according to Rita."

I said, "Is that true?"

"No, not at all. Well, Pat may have a crush on me, but I don't have one on her and never will. She's not my type. Rita and I started a verbal fight about Rita's suspicions, and it got out of hand, so they asked us to leave the club. When we drove home, we continued the fight, and before I knew it, Rita's fist hit my face. My nose was bleeding, and on top of that, I have a black eye. I am now unable to show up at work. I would not be allowed in the mansion. Gina would send me home in this condition. I'm sure you can understand?"

I was sitting in my chair rigid and in shock. The first words I spoke were when Marianne said, "Are you there, Chantal?"

I murmured, "Yes, I am, but I'm in shock. Did Rita apologize to you when she hit you in the face?"

Marianne answered quickly, "Yes, she did. She said she didn't know what had come over her, and the thought of losing me was overwhelming and stronger than she had anticipated.

"She is very upset with herself right now and constantly asking me to forgive her reaction that night. I know it was in a jealous rage, and she was a bit tipsy at the time, but I told her this could only happen once. The second time, I would pack up and leave her without hesitation."

I said, "I hope she understands that you will do what you said. There is no reason good enough to slap someone you love, or anyone for that matter. Do you hear what I'm saying, Marianne?"

"Yes, Chantal, I hear and agree with you 100%. While I'm home, and until I'm presentable again, I will look for another job. I don't think I will return to Topaz. Three years is enough. I am tired of the entire charade. I will let Gina know once I have found something else."

I thought: *Finally, common sense is taking over.*

On Thursday, I got a call from Marianne. She said, "Chantal, I got another job opportunity."

I was excited to hear where she had found a job so quickly. She sounded bubbly and told me she could work at a bar as bartender, be her own boss (besides the owner of the establishment), and earn 50% of the drinks she sold to the customers. "The best thing of all is no sex involved, isn't that great?"

I thought: *Here we go again.*

I answered, "Is Rita okay with that?

She said, "Yes, way more than the Topaz business."

"When do you start?"

Marianne laughed and said, "When my eye is healed, sometime after the holidays."

I asked, "Is everything all right between you and Rita now?"

She said, "Yes, she has cooled off, but is till angry at herself for doing what she did."

I answered, "As long as she remembers not to do that again; that's all that matters."

I wouldn't call Marianne till the week she would start the new job. I just wanted to take some time for myself and went to the Blue Note that weekend danced and flirted the night away.

However, Marianne was still in the background. It felt like I could not shake her off me. She was like a sister, and I loved her for who she was. And I had promised Enzo I would watch over her, which for sure I would do, with or without Rita's approval.

December 24 came fast and with some freezing weather and snow as well. I went to Mom's house for the wonderful meal she always prepared. The table was covered with food and wine. Later in the evening, after our delicious meal and coffee and cake, it was time to unwrap the gifts. I had bought my mom a wool sweater in the blue marine colour she liked. My stepdad got a gift card to buy food for his expensive saltwater fish. They bought me a new scarf and gloves – aquamarine blue, my favourite colour. I could use them right away as the weather was cold enough. It was a wonderful evening. I felt blessed to have my family by my side.

CHAPTER 17

Two days later, I called my mom and asked her if she would like to go on a vacation with me – a short 4-day trip somewhere warm from December 27–30. She was thrilled and wasted no time packing light clothes since I had said the word "warm". I looked forward to going to the Canary Islands in Tenerife, Spain, where I knew the weather was always sunny and warm during our wintertime. Plus, they had great food. We loved baking in the sun, and having our sangria on ice in the afternoon. I booked a last-minute flight after I had permission from my boss Paul. The restaurant was closed anyway from December 24–January 2nd. I called Marianne, but I got her answering machine, so I told her I was leaving for a few days with my mom and would call her when I got back.

We left on a Wednesday morning to return on Sunday evening. On the plane, we already had a lot to talk about. We had a drink and chatted away. The flight was only 4 hours and flew by. Upon arriving, a shuttle bus picked us up and drove us to our 5-star hotel. I knew the hotel was first class, and I wanted to treat my mother with the best – and let's say myself too. We were warmly welcomed and felt somewhat like VIP. We only wanted to have fun and some well-deserved rest for both of us.

That afternoon, we baked in the sun on the terrace from the hotel, and yes, you guessed it, we had a pitcher of sangria on ice on the table. It was so wonderful being with my mom, just the two of us. While talking about things that were going on in her and my life, she asked me out of the blue if I had been with a man lately or was interested in anyone. I shook my head and laughed, "No Mom, nothing on the horizon yet. I just want to stay alone for now, and I will let you know if Mr. Wonderful arrives." We both laughed so loud that other guests laughed with us.

The four days went by so quickly. We had a lot of fun. The last night before we returned home, we were at a bar and my mom was a little tipsy. She started to sing along with another male customer like Pavarotti. It was like a duet in an opera. It brought tears to my eyes seeing her so happy.

We had to do this more often. How many of my friends could say they could go on a vacation with their mother and have a blast? I could not think of no one, but me. I was blessed to have a mother who loved to do the things that I loved to do. We were not only mother and daughter, but best buddies.

On the flight back home, my mind drifted away, and I wondered what Marianne was up to. Upon arriving at Charles de Gaulle Airport, I drove my mother home. I stayed about one hour with her to have a coffee and tell my stepfather what a good time we had. He loved to hear our stories, but was happy to have my mom home again. He had missed her cooking, and I didn't blame him…

Since it was Sunday evening, I thought I'd give Marianne a quick call, hoping she would be home. I just needed to know how things were going with her and Rita. Marianne picked up the phone. I said, "Hey Sis, it's me, Chantal."

She yelled, "Welcome back. I missed you. When do I see you?"

I answered, "Well, tomorrow night is our planned night. Remember it's Dec 31, and we are going out. Are things still as planned?"

"For sure, she said. "We have made reservations at the best restaurant, and after that, we'll go to a private party. Is that okay?"

I answered, "Yes, that sounds wonderful."

I asked her, "How are things with you and Rita?"

She said, "All is well between us. I still work at Topaz while I think about letting go of the job there to accept the new one. A few days ago, I contracted a venereal disease from a customer who I have known for 2 years and who is married. Therefore, I didn't use protection because I trusted him. Stupid me," she added.

I almost wanted to slap her face when I heard that. Good thing I was on the phone. Instead, she heard a long sigh. She continued, "But Chantal, don't worry, I have it under control. I'm on medication, and it will be all over soon. I spoke to Gina, the owner, who told me not to work until I was disease-free. At the same time, I told her I was going to quit anyway. Gina froze when I said I was going to quit. She pleaded with me, and said, 'Where else do you think you can make this kind of money? Please reconsider your decision because once you're out, there is no return. That's the rule.'"

I said, "And are you sticking with your decision?"

Marianne answered, "Yes, I won't go back there anymore. Rita has asked me for so long to let go of my job at Topaz, and the disease was the last straw."

Marianne heard a sigh of relief. I said, "Well, I'm glad for you. It's time, don't you think?"

Marianne started to laugh, and said, "Chantal, I'll see you tomorrow evening, let's say 6 pm, and we will continue our conversation." We hung up the phone. I was happy to know she would be leaving Topaz for good.

On December 31, I drove to Rita's house. The girls were waiting for me all dressed up. Rita was dressed in a black and grey tuxedo without the bow, while Marianne was wearing a long blue silky dress that matched the colour of her eyes and showed off her gorgeous and sexy silhouette she looked radiant. I had made the decision to be comfortable that night, black leather pants with a red blouse tucked in and leather black belt with a buckle showing my initial "C". I could have looked almost like a tomboy, if it weren't for my long hair.

We headed off in Rita's car to a French restaurant called Les Trois Arches, which was close to the Eiffel Tower. It very classy and had a wonderful atmosphere. The food was a set menu, but it was top quality – oyster's au gratin as a starter, chateaubriand with pommes frites and asparagus sautéed in butter, with chocolate mousse to finish it all off. In between, the wine was flowing like Canada's wonder site Niagara Falls. Marianne didn't talk about her next move. This was not the right time, I guessed. It was party time.

We had a perfect dinner; the restaurant was a good choice by my friends. I owed them, since it was all pre-paid. I did not have to bring out my wallet. I shook my head sideways and thanked them both. Marianne said, "And now sweetie, we are going to the club for a private party. Their doors are closed. Only invited guests will be allowed in. Let's go girls."

At the club was a close-knit group of invitees. I saw different faces and many well-dressed, high-class girls. *How did my friends know them?* I wondered. They didn't. The owners knew them all and had invited them. The music was loud, and everyone was in the mood for drinking and dancing; so were we. I had a girl watching me as if she wanted to undress me. I pretended not to notice it and danced the night away with Rita and Marianne. Then the lights went out, and we heard 12 strikes of something that sounded like England's Big Ben." Denise and Pat had especially installed it, so we could enter 1973 with a bang.

We shouted, "Happy New Year" together. Marianne and Rita kissed each other and then it was my turn. We hugged each other and said, "Let's do this for many years to come." Which we did. "Happy New Year my friends."

We left separately around 1:30 am. I said good-bye to both. I called a taxi to drive me to Rita's house. There, I got into my car and drove home very slowly. I was slightly tipsy, but not drunk enough to be scared to drive.

I called my mom and stepdad to wish them a "Happy New Year". I knew they would watch television till they had enough of the programs. Mom was glad I had a good time with my friends and that I had made it home safely at a decent hour. I was tired and needed my bed. I would know in the next day or two when Rita and Marianne went home.

"Good night, Mom. I love you both," I whispered in the phone. Then I fell into bed like a log.

CHAPTER 18

On Wednesday, January 2, the day could not go fast enough for me; the restaurant would re-open the next day. I was ready to see Marianne and Rita and hear what she had in store for her next job and everything else in their lives. I drove to Rita's home, where the door swung open before I could ring the doorbell. Marianne squeezed me in her arms, while Rita looked over her shoulder and smiled.

I hugged Rita who guided me inside, and we all took a seat in her living room, where chilled wine was waiting for us. Full to the rim, we held our glasses high, and they both said, "Welcome friend and again Happy New Year." They still didn't know how my trip with my mom had been. They mentioned how good I looked. I said, "Well, I needed the sunshine I guess. And Spain is always the best place in winter. I needed to tan to celebrate 1973…with you girls."

The night went quickly as we had so much to talk about. They had a wonderful time and had gone home from the party at 5 am, Marianne told me. While Rita was in the kitchen, Marianne told me all about the new girls she met at the party. They were all lesbian ladies with a partner from wealthy families, very classy.

Rita's kitchen door swung open and she brought in a delicious-smelling casserole of stew. "Okay you two," she said, "let's eat. I'm starving."

We had a good meal cooked by Rita – beef stew with mushrooms and homemade baguette. She knew I liked that bread and dipping it in the beef sauce. I gave her a compliment on the tender beef stew and the crispy bread, and for the first time it made her blush. I had never seen that before.

While relaxing after dinner in one of the couches, I asked Marianne what her next step was now that she no longer worked at Topaz. She hesitated for a second, looked at Rita, and said, Well, like I told you before, I had another job offer at a bar, but I decided not to take it. I don't want to work for another boss anymore and make them rich."

I am going to work for myself. My look (with a question mark) must have been visible to both when Marianne said quickly, "I am going to work from home. Before I left Topaz, I gave my best and most reliable wealthy customers our address." She looked at Rita for confirmation. "I told them to contact me in about 3 weeks. I had to get organized first, and told them I was willing to see them in 'private' at my house if they wanted to see me."

I looked at Rita and said, "Are you okay with that, dear?"

She said, "Yes, we will try and see if it works. First of all, it's safer, and the money is 100% ours. We would like to buy a house together very soon, and this way we may just succeed in a short period of time. I was a bit in shock, but buying a house would indeed go faster with Rita's income and Marianne keeping 100% of the money. But it was still a risky business.

"What about the neighbours?" I asked. "Marianne, are you sure that's going to work?"

"We'll see," she said. "In the meantime, I'll get things organized and see what happens. Rita already requested and was approved to work part-time at the accounting firm. She wants to stay close to me whenever I have a client over."

Rita said, "I will stay in another room next to where Marianne is pampering the client. Maybe there will be sex involved, but protection will be readily available. If the client refuses, then he's out the door. Those are the rules." She and Marianne high-fived, while my brain tried to come to grips with this weird idea.

I said, "Well, let's hope it works for both of you."

Days went by. I didn't want to call Marianne too often. I knew she had to get "organized" for her not-so-new career. She needed to plan to make sure the neighbours wouldn't become suspicious and to make sure nothing else would hamper their plan of receiving wealthy businessmen in their home. I was saddened that Rita did nothing to lead Marianne into a different direction of work. Was this real love? Or was it greed?

A few weeks after our last get together, I got a call from Marianne. She said everything had worked out well so far. She was making good money. The only thing that hadn't been in her plan was that Rita did not allow her to spend too much time with her client and demanded she explain what they did and why it took her so long, etc.

"As you know, Chantal, she is very jealous but also controlling. I don't know if it will last between us this way. We love each other, but I'm afraid the jealousy will kill our relationship and all our plans we have for the future. I'm not getting any younger, you know."

"Yes, Marianne." I added, "We all getting a little older every day. You just have to be careful with how you handle things between you and Rita. I don't want anything to happen to you. Do you hear me?"

She laughed, but I could hear a slight tremble of fear in her voice. She said, "Don't worry, I'll take care of myself and try not to let things get out of hand."

I asked her what she did when she had no customers to entertain. She bluntly said, "I have a few glasses of wine until I feel tipsy. Then I listen to some music and try to figure out what my life will be like 10 years from now. Sometimes I call my mother to talk and listen to her wise advice."

"Well, that's good if that works for you," I told her. "But my dear friend," I said, "I have to go now and will be in touch soon."

CHAPTER 19

After we hung up, I thought I was not convinced that everything was going so well at Marianne and Rita's place with the "work from home idea". They may have a fat bank account between them, but Rita's jealous outbursts were not something that would sit well with Marianne, who was (by choice) a self-made, independent, strong-willed girl before she met Rita.

I was wondering what, if anything, I could do. Maybe I should pop in to say hello more often, but Marianne's working-from-home schedule made this idea almost impossible.

About a week after we had last spoken, I got a call in the middle of the night from Rita. She yelled in a panic that Marianne's skin felt cold while they were in bed and she could not wake her up. She said after she had come back from the bathroom and snuggled up against Marianne's body, it felt cold and damp. She had jumped out of bed and tried to wake her.

I said, "Call an ambulance right now. I'll be there in 5 minutes." Wide awake now and dressed like a slob, I jumped in my car and sped through red lights. I even got there before the ambulance.

Rita opened the door. I ran upstairs and saw Marianne in bed. She was cold but still breathing. Her lips were blue and her face was a pale grey. She looked lifeless. If I hadn't been able to see her shallow breathing, I would have thought she was dead. While I starred at her in disbelief, tears started rolling down my cheeks. Then the ambulance arrived. They quickly put an oxygen mask on her and asked Rita if Marianne had any allergies or had taken medication. She showed them an empty sleeping pill container (which they took with them as they left) and said she could not remember how many were in it before they went to bed the night before.

The paramedics put Marianne on a stretcher, loaded her into the waiting ambulance, and sped off to the hospital. I drove behind the ambulance, with Rita next to me; she was in no mood to drive a car. She cried uncontrollably all the way to the hospital. I knew something must have triggered Marianne to empty the bottle of sleeping pills, but this was not the time to talk about it. I just hoped and prayed that they could save her life; that's all I could think about right now.

Arriving at the hospital, we quickly parked the car at the emergency parking spot and followed the paramedics inside. Rita had to give the nurse some information about Marianne because in all the panic she hadn't taken any of Marianne's papers and ID. Fortunately, that seemed not to be a problem at that given time. We asked where they were taking Marianne once the paramedics pushed the stretcher through the doors that said, "no visitors" allowed. The nurse said, "We will bring her to the operating/evaluation room to evaluate her condition and do the necessary procedures to help her. Just have a seat. "We will call you when we know more."

We each sank into one of the hard hospital chairs, holding each other's hand. Rita was shivering like a willow tree, tears were rolling down her cheeks. She said, "Chantal, it's all my fault. I'm the one who fell in love with her. I'm the one who made her leave her boyfriend, and I'm to blame for letting her do what she wanted to do in my house. I'm the one who goes crazy when she's with a man even if I'm there. I just can't stand it."

I looked at Rita feeling somewhat sorry for her. At least she was honest and felt overwhelmingly guilty. I told her not to take all the blame herself. I whispered close to her ear, "Marianne also loves you, and she would not have left Enzo if she didn't think you were the one. She told me she could not imagine life without you after she met you at the club, Rita."

She looked at me and hugged me, thanking me for giving her strength and believing in both of them. I didn't dare ask Rita what had gone wrong the night before. I would figure it out later. My focus was on Marianne, who was struggling in the OR. After 20 minutes, I could not hold myself back any longer. I stood up and asked the nurse if she had any news for us. She told me that the doctors had to empty out the contents of Marianne's stomach, and she was out of danger. "However," she added, "you will still have to wait to see her until they bring her out of the operating room. I will let you know when that happens and what room number she'll be in."

CHAPTER 20

Rita and I hugged and cried at the same time. Feelings of relief and tiredness set in – after all, it was now 5 am in the morning. I went to a pay phone in the hospital's hallway and left a message for my boss. I was not going in today; that much I knew. I felt like I had been run over by a bus. The nurse came to see us 30 minutes later and guided us to room number 21.

Marianne lay under white bed sheets. She looked like an angel. She was as pale as the sheets, except her raven-black hair surrounded her face on the pillows. Rita spoke softly and asked how she was feeling. Marianne opened her eyes slightly, looked at both of us, and smiled. She whispered, "I'm okay. I guess I'm glad to see you both. I'm tired and think I will fall asleep any minute now. Maybe come back tomorrow. I will be all better, okay girls?

We agreed to leave her alone and kissed her on her forehead. While Rita stepped out of the room, I quickly said to Marianne, "Don't you ever scare me again like that! Do you understand! She had an "I'm sorry" look on her face and shook her head, whispering she wouldn't. I left the room and drove Rita home.

She asked me to come in for coffee, which I for sure needed. She made breakfast for both of us. While she was in the kitchen, I reflected on what had happened between them. *What could have driven Marianne to take her own life?* I wondered. Rita and I did not talk much while eating breakfast and drinking our espresso. However, I needed to know a little bit more about the situation before I would go home.

We cleaned up and sank into the couch. I said, "Rita why did you tell me at the hospital what happened to Marianne was your fault?"

She looked at me and said, "Well, I have the feeling that Marianne is not happy anymore, and I think it's me she's not happy with."

I shook my head and said, "Maybe Marianne is tired of fighting, and maybe you are somewhat overly controlling and jealous, but don't forget she is a very independent girl. She always was and always will be. Maybe you must lay low for a while and figure out together with her when she's back home what's bothering her and what's bothering you. Don't you think that's an idea?"

Rita answered, "Yes, you're right, Chantal. As soon as she comes home from the hospital, we will talk about the future and how she sees it. I'll do anything for Marianne; I want her happy and content. I love her deeply. I never want this to happen again, ever."

I agreed with her statement. This was my first experience with a close friend trying to commit suicide. It was especially hard with Marianne, who was so lively. I had thought she loved life and everything that came with it.

So, I insisted again and told Rita, "Talk it over when she's home, and if there's anything I can do, call me. If you feel it's getting out of hand, keep your cool, and think what she did last night. She thought it was her only way out. However, it was the wrong way out. That can not happen again." Rita agreed 100% with me. From what her body language and facial expression told me, she was very sad.

CHAPTER 21

The next morning before I had to go to work, I drove to the hospital. Rita had beaten me to it and was sitting on the bedside near Marianne, holding hands. I pushed her away a few inches and hugged Marianne, who looked a lot better. Rita pulled a chair next to the other side of the bed, so we each flanked Marianne's bed. I asked how she was.

She said, "Well, it looks like I can go home this afternoon, to Rita's relief and mine." Marianne also added that she had to give a statement to the doctors and police as to why she wanted to commit suicide. "I knew that was going to happen. When someone tries to take their own life, the police want to know the reason behind it."

I asked, "Did you tell them the truth? And by the way, *why* did you do this stupid thing?"

Marianne looked sheepishly at me and turned her eyes to Rita. She said, "I told them what I told Rita the night before. I said I was depressed and had too many fights with my partner. I could no longer stand it and wanted to end my life."

There it was. Rita looked at me and rolled her eyes. She looked at Marianne, kissed her, and said, "From now on, everything will be better. I promise you, my angel. I'll do anything to keep our relationship healthy. There will be no more fights and no more shouting. If there's a problem, we'll sit down and talk about it. I will do my best not to be so jealous anymore. You know my heart belongs to you, and I know your heart is mine, and there is no need to deny it."

I sat there stone-faced, waiting for Marianne's reply. She smiled at me and said, "Chantal, you witnessed this, okay?"

We all laughed, while I said, "Yes, I will be the middleman or woman if I have to, just call me, and I will be over in no time. Just never give us a reason to call the ambulance again. I never want you, Marianne, to do anything like this again, all right?

"But now ladies, I have to go to work. If you're okay with it, I'll pop in after work."

They both agreed. Rita said, "Dinner will be waiting for you, my friend." I hugged Rita and Marianne and left. A feeling of relief came over me, knowing that my best friend, who had just tried to take her own life, had been saved, and everything would be better from now on. However, I would keep a closer eye on both from here on.

In the afternoon, I got a call from Enzo. Bad news travels fast, and he had heard that Marianne was in the hospital and had tried to commit suicide. He asked me if that was true. How could I tell him a lie? He had the right to know. I said, "Yes, Enzo, that's what happened, but she is out of danger now. She can go home later today."

The poor guy. Clearly emotional, he whispered, "Why did she do this? Was it that woman that drove her over the edge? I don't see any other reason."

I told him it was a combination of things, but also that Rita was overly jealous of Marianne, and they had many fights since they lived together. I said, "Enzo, listen to me, I don't live together with them, but I can assure you I will keep a closer eye on what's going on there. I promise you.

"I was as shocked as you are when Rita called to tell me that Marianne lay cold and lifeless next to her in bed. I was at their house in a blink of an eye, while the ambulance was on the way. I don't want this to happen again. I will keep you posted during the next few days, all right my friend?"

Enzo thanked me for the update on the former love of his life and told me I was a good friend. He said, "Come by the restaurant one day, and I'll make something special for you on the house."

I told him, "You can count on that, Enzo."

What a nice guy he was. I wondered if Marianne had any regrets about leaving him for Rita. But I was not about to ask her that question. Time would tell.

That evening I drove to Marianne's house. She opened the door, and we stood there for about 2 minutes holding each other. She felt so frail. It looked like she could use a good juicy steak. Rita called us into the house, and said, "Hey guys, dinner is about to be served."

I wiped away a few tears from my cheeks – "tears of joy" I called them. I was happy to see my friend alive and well. We toasted with a glass of red wine to the health of Rita's lover and my best friend Marianne. We had a good evening. We did not bring up what had happened a few days earlier. I thought that was to be discussed between the two of them.

I would sit down with Marianne one of these days when Rita was working and talk about it then. I did see some sadness in Marianne's eyes at certain moments. Was she sad because the suicide attempt had failed, or did she still think about Enzo? I needed to find out soon what was bothering her.

CHAPTER 22

Marianne was approaching 32, as was I. The years had flown by like it was yesterday.

They had lots of parties at their house with gay and Lesbian friends. They were all very friendly and accepted me for who I was. After all, I was their host's best friend. Marianne drank a lot more than I had ever seen before at those parties. She even mildly flirted with her good-looking gay friends under the watchful eye of Rita, who I think did not mind her behaviour while tipsy. After a few hours, Marianne waved at me to come with her to the back yard. I took my glass of wine and joined her. We sat down on one of the benches between the lush green bushes and flowers. I asked her what was it she wanted to see me about.

She started crying and said, "I want a child in my life. I have the urge to become a mother. My instinct is taking over. I need a child to make my life complete. Do you understand that, Chantal? Is it normal to be a lesbian and want to have a baby?"

I sat there speechless for a few seconds and then reassured her it was totally normal. I said, "You are almost 32 years old and a normal female. Even if you live with a lesbian woman, your female instinct stays the same as any other girl's, like me…"

She hugged me, crying even more. She whispered that I was so understanding, and she had complete trust in me. She then said, "How and where can I find a man who is willing to make me pregnant? The urge is so great I can't stand it much longer."

We plotted a way to find a man who was willing to donate his sperm. In the event that this didn't work, she said she would go to bed with one of her most-liked clients and have unprotected sex on a regular basis, without Rita involved. I told Marianne this would not go well if Rita found out her plans and wasn't involved. She had to tell her about the urge to have a baby, as soon as they were alone and *sober*.

Two days later after work, I drove to Marianne's house to say hi and find out if the two had spoken about Marianne wanting a child. Marianne was still alone at home. Rita would arrive later from work. I nestled myself in one of the couches and asked my friend if she had talked with Rita about wanting a baby.

She asked me if I wanted a drink. I said, "Yes, sure a drink would be great – an espresso with a small cognac." After all, I was done working and only wanted to be with my friend, who was in an emotional turmoil now. Marianne came back with the same drink for both of us. It looked like she too could use a stiff drink.

So, I asked again, "Did you finally talk to Rita about what you want so badly in your life?"

Marianne sadly answered, "Yes, I did, but Rita thinks it's not a good idea. She doesn't feel the need to have a child around us, and what would people say about a lesbian couple having a baby? That's unheard of!

"I could not convince her; I talked for hours on end. And finally, I told her she didn't love me enough and didn't give a damn how I felt. I said that she wasn't a real woman with feminine feelings. We were totally opposite; maybe we didn't belong to each other. I would rather leave her to live on my own and have that baby I want so much than stay with an ignorant woman."

I said, "What did she say when you told her all that? She must have been flabbergasted, no?" I took my drink and finished it in one shot. Knowing what was to come, I asked Marianne to pour us another drink and have a few crackers on the side. I could not wait to hear how Rita had reacted. Marianne came back with my drink and another one for herself, along with cheese crackers and some nuts.

She immediately said, "Rita was in shock when I told her I would leave her if she would not agree to have a child in our lives. I told her exactly what was missing in my life to be happy and complete, and that I would not stop until I was pregnant with or without her permission."

"Wow, Marianne that was right to the point. Good job. That's how you do it. And how long did you give her to reflect on your decision?"

"Well, I told Rita to give me the green light in 10 days, or I would be out of here." We started laughing with the green light, as if Marianne stood on a street waiting for the lights to turn from red to Green – funny.

A few minutes later, we heard the key turning in the door lock. The door swung open and Rita came straight towards us, hugging Marianne first and then giving me a bear hug too. "Hi guys, what's up?"

I said, "I only came by to say hi and have a nice drink to keep my friend company till you got here. I'm on my way home now. You both have a nice evening, and talk to you soon." Rita did not make any attempt to have me stay for dinner, and I was not in the mood to stay either. They had lots to talk about, and I wasn't needed in that conversation.

CHAPTER 23

I drove home that same weekend. I hadn't been there in a while and craved my mother's cooking. She was happy to see me and had all kind of questions about what was going on in my life. So after dinner, I slowly introduced my friend Marianne to her and started from the beginning when met at the disco. I left out some hot details about her real job, but told her about Enzo and Rita, whom she had met at a club for woman only. My mom was not at all surprised that things like that happened in someone's life. She knew of a woman who left her husband with her two kids for another woman, so this was nothing new.

I was relieved she knew someone like that. She even said her hairdresser was gay and had two children. While he was still married to his wife, she was okay with him being gay. They stayed together for the sake of the kids and the business.

Really, my mom knew a lot more than I anticipated. She was very up to date about things that I thought were left unsaid and in the dark by her generation. I loved that my mom was so open and not judgmental. She was a down-to-earth woman, and the best cook in town.

On a Thursday that same week, Marianne called me and asked if there was a vacant apartment for rent in the building where I lived. I was stunned and said, "As a matter of fact, yes, there is one on the 7th floor – a one bedroom with a balcony. Why? What's going on?"

She said she couldn't wait any longer for an answer from Rita and wanted to move out as soon as possible. "I want to teach her a lesson and tell her that I don't need her to fulfill my life, and she can't dictate what I can or cannot do. I left her a note."

I understood and was ready to help my friend with whatever she needed. This was serious. I called the landlord to organize the move for Marianne and do the rental paperwork. I told him it would only be short term.

That same week on a Friday, while Rita was at work, Marianne and I rented a truck and moved all the stuff that belonged to her. Marianne was happy as a bird, when she entered her own little cozy apartment, right above her best friend. Me…

We did go out that evening for a quick dinner and were wondering how long it would take for Rita to contact her. Marianne was in a good mood and didn't care about Rita at that given moment. That same evening after work, Rita found Marianne's note saying she had moved away until Rita agreed to let her have a baby; only then she would return home to Rita.

It didn't take long for Rita to call me. Marianne and I had just got back home from dinner. She asked me if I knew where Marianne had moved to or where she was.

I told her she was on the 7th floor in my building. Marianne had agreed I could tell Rita where she was. There was no secret and no hiding on her part. Rita asked me why she had done this. I said, "You will have to talk to her about the *why*. I'm just her friend, and you are her lover and should know more than me! Think hard. Maybe why she moved out will come to you."

It didn't take long for Rita to arrive at the address where I and now Marianne lived. She didn't bother to stop by my apartment and went straight to the 7th floor. Marianne was waiting for her. They had agreed to talk and try to resolve the problem while it was still not too late. If Rita agreed to Marianne's wishes to have a child, I thought they would end up living happily ever after together in Rita's house again. After a few hours, Rita left, and Marianne called me to come up and see her. It was fun not to have to take my car; I only had to take the elevator to the 7th floor. I loved it.

She welcomed me with open arms as usual. I could see she had been crying; her eyes were swollen and red. I sat down next to her on the sofa and put my arms around her. I knew she needed a hug. She looked at me with those sad eyes, and said, "I need your advice, Chantal."

I told her I was all ears and wanted nothing more than to help her.

She continued and said she was going to organize a party with gay and lesbian friends the next weekend. Rita was welcome if she wanted to come. She said, "I am going to try and find one of my gay friends to be a sperm donor."

I was stunned. I asked her how she came up with that idea. She said, "Well, I have heard there is now a method to insert live sperm that's collected from a male donor into the vagina. It's used for women who have difficulty becoming pregnant. It's called In-Vitro Fertilization or IVF for short.

I was aware of that method, but who would she ask to participate? She said, "You remember those two good-looking gay guys, Bruno and Daniel? They are young and very loving men."

I said, Yes, I know who they are."

"Well, I am going to ask if one of them is willing to donate sperm for me to become pregnant. I will tell them I want this baby so badly, and they are my choice because they are such a nice loving couple.

"What do you think, Chantal? Is that a good idea?"

I said, "Well, it's worth the try. The only thing is if they will accept and if Rita will agree."

Marianne added, "I don't care if Rita agrees or not. It's my decision and Bruno or Daniel will have to agree first. I don't mind raising a child on my own. I'll find another partner if Rita does not want to see me anymore. At this given moment, Rita will have to give in, or she's out of my life and she knows it all too well.

"I've saved enough money to get by for a long time without working. And the work I did, well, I will give that all up when I have a child. As a matter of fact, I don't want to see any man currently. I have had enough of it. I don't want anyone to touch me, especially living on the 7th floor of a building next to my best friend. I wouldn't want the elevator to go up and down 5 times a day to my place." That was hilarious, and we started laughing out loud at that statement and high fived. "I'll become a mother first and find a job as a waitress, just like I did before."

That was joy and music to my ears.

CHAPTER 24

That following weekend, Marianne invited some of her closest friends to her place, including Bruno and Daniel, who had lived together more than 10 years. I watched them together interacting with everyone. They were such a loving couple and good-looking. Marianne was right: If one of them agreed to donate his sperm, the baby would be gorgeous.

I started giggling with my thoughts. I already saw myself as the baby's godmother. Rita was also attending the party. She did not want to miss out on anything Marianne was doing and wanted to keep an eye on her. She was still somewhat controlling as she had always been.

I saw Marianne standing close to Bruno and Daniel, feeding them with all kind of goodies, and filling their glasses with wine. I knew she would strike and ask them the question when they both were settled in. After all, this was a tiny apartment, and everyone had questions about why she had moved here.

Her answer was always the same. "I needed the space on my own for a while." All her friends knew by now that she had tried to take her own life a month ago and were not at all surprised with her answer. Rita joined in on occasion when Marianne had a conversation with someone, but left her alone most of the time she was there. She knew it would be difficult to get Marianne's attention for herself, let alone convince her to come back home and live with her.

A few hours into the party, I saw Marianne inviting Bruno and Daniel to her tiny balcony away from the chatting crowd. I stayed inside. I didn't want to interrupt. I knew why she wanted both men alone outside. I made sure no one joined them and kept Rita at bay.

I walked towards Rita and asked her how she was doing. She looked at me and said, "I don't know anymore what to do to get Marianne back into my life."

I smiled and said, "You know very well what Marianne wants in her life besides you, and there's nothing wrong with wanting a child in hers and your life.

"You may not want to get pregnant. I understand that, but it's Marianne's right to want a baby. That's her desire and a mother's instinct. I don't think you can stop that, or you will lose her forever. I promise you that."

Rita looked at me, shaking her head yes. She said, "You're right as always. I will have to give in because I can't live without her. I know that now."

I thought finally common sense had come out of her mouth. I hugged her and said, "Listen it will all come together as long as you are willing to satisfy your partner, and maybe you will enjoy the baby more than you know. You will be a real close-knit family. If Marianne feels there is a missing link in her life, and that link is a child, then let her have one."

Rita agreed once again with me. At that same moment, Marianne and the two guys came back inside. Marianne was all smiles. I knew she must have had a good answer from either one of the men. She came straight to me while Rita was still standing next to me. She pulled me aside and told me Daniel was willing to donate his sperm on the condition she didn't tell anyone he was the biological father. There she said it. I already knew who the biological dad would be. She also knew I would not tell a soul. I grabbed and hugged her. We were both ecstatic. The party came to an end later than expected, but by two in the morning everyone had left except Rita and me.

This was the moment Marianne would tell Rita of her plan, without mentioning who would donate the sperm. I saw Rita getting all red in the face, but also shaking her head agreeing with Marianne's plan.

She hugged her long-time partner and kissed her passionately, while I watched and smiled. I thanked God for this critical moment and the acceptance from Rita to make Marianne happy. I think my conversation with Rita must have opened her heart and mind.

In the same week, Marianne went home to see her mom and family. They were very surprised and happy to see her. Her family knew Marianne was living with a girl, but thought they were more like roommates. She told her mom she had met this guy, and they were talking about having a baby together. However, she would not marry him, and he had agreed to that.

Marianne was ready to have a child in her life as she was pushing early-thirties. She talked about how Daniel was so handsome, and the baby would be so cute. She was all bubbly and excited when talking to her mom, who had been flabbergasted when she said, "I'm not going to marry him because of the baby. I can take care of the baby without having a man around the house. We don't live together anyway at this time."

Marianne's mom was all excited for her and welcomed the idea of having a grandchild in her life. She did not hesitate to take her daughter in her arms and embraced her warmly. She said, "You go ahead, sweetie.

Whatever makes you happy, then I'm happy." Marianne was all smiles and glad her mom understood.

However, she felt a bit sad she had not been honest with her mom about the way she would have the baby. But she could finally prepare herself for the procedure that had to take place, without having to worry and explain the real situation to her family just yet. Telling her family, the other part about Rita being her lover would come later. By then, her mom would be a grandmother and would forgive her for loving a woman and needing Daniel's input as the sperm donor.

CHAPTER 25

Now Rita had to tell her family about the decision to extend her own family and Marianne wanting to have a baby. Rita's family knew Marianne was Rita's long-time partner. They were not at all surprised about Marianne's desire to become a mother; after all, she wasn't born as a lesbian. She just fell in love with a lesbian woman and had left the man behind with whom she had spent 5 years of her life.

Rita, on the other hand, had masculine tendencies since she was a child, and it had been obvious that she liked women rather than men from an early age.

Rita's mother was very pleased with the idea. That way she would become a grandmother, which she had never dreamed of before. To Rita's relief, they opened a bottle of wine and toasted to the wonderful news.

Marianne kept her word. No more sexual favours with men from now on. The sex shop forever closed its doors. She was only focused on having a baby. I was very excited for her; it felt like I was going to have that baby…

Almost every day I had to call Marianne, who now had moved back in with Rita. She said the love life with Rita was back on fire, like in the sexy old days when they first met. Since Marianne was no longer seeing men for paid sexual affairs, Rita was all over her. She kissed her tenderly all over her beautiful body, whispering how much she loved her and how beautiful she was while caressing and stroking her between her legs, making sure she could not escape having an orgasm. She conquered her heart all over again.

Rita knew how to make her Marianne happy. She swore to her she would never provoke another fight with her, lay a hand on her, or make her feel like a million-dollar whore, who fucked men for money. Marianne said, "From now on we are one. And soon we will be three, and I am looking forward to that happening."

I took a deep breath and said, "Wow, that's a whole lot different than a few months ago, don't you think?"

Marianne answered, "Yes, and it's a wonderful feeling."

I asked her when she would see Daniel and the doctor who would arrange to have the In-Vitro Fertilization done. She answered, "Next week Wednesday. I will let you know. It's only an appointment to talk about the way it will be done and when. I have to see my family doctor first. We will be told what Daniel must do and my part to make it work. We don't have all the details yet, but I'll keep you posted, my friend. You can count on that."

Oh, I was sure she would include me in all the details. I couldn't wait.

Three weekends went by and on Thursday morning, the phone rang. It was Marianne. She sounded overjoyed and said, "Chantal, it's done. The deal is done, and the appointment with the gynecologist for the procedure is confirmed for next week. I've been watching my ovulation for more than a month now. My family doctor told me this was mandatory for the IVF.

"I had to take some fertility drugs to stimulate the ovaries to produce several eggs – not just one or a few per month as we normally have. Next week, they will retrieve the eggs from my body. It's a minor surgery. I may have some cramping, but it will not last long. Then the insemination, as they call it, will be done with Daniel's sperm and my eggs mixed together. The eggs and sperm are stored in a controlled chamber. As per my doctor, the sperm most often enters the egg a few hours after insemination. If the doctor thinks the chance of fertilization is low considering my age, the sperm will be injected directly into the eggs that I carry.

"We will see how they are going to do this. I can tell you, Chantal, that it's not for free. It may cost us between $5000 and $8,000 but I'm so ready to be a mother. My friend, you have no idea."

I couldn't hold my tears back and replied, "Yes, I do have an idea how happy you are and what wonderful news this is."

I asked her when she had to be at the hospital. She said next Thursday. "We have to be there at 8:30 am, are you coming too?"

"Of course, I will. I want to be there for you. And Rita is coming, I assume?"

"Yes," she said, "Rita will be there as well. I'm so happy, Chantal." We both laughed and cried at the same time. All bubbly and full of excitement she said, Bruno and Daniel will be there too.

"They will be in a different and very private location while they retrieve my eggs and prepare me to receive Daniel's donation. I pray Daniel's gift of life and my eggs will get together and *hatch*...." She laughed. "After all that, hopefully the baby start growing inside of me without hesitation." Now we both were laughing a bit hysterically and nervously at the same time. "I'm so excited I have no words for it.

"The doctor also said it's possible with multiple spermatozoids that I could have twins or triplets. Wouldn't that be fantastic, Chantal?"

"Of course, that would be. I would love to be the godmother for your baby or twins… what do you think about that?"

She immediately said, "Of course, who better then you? I already thought of asking you. I spoke about it with my mom, and she agreed that you would be great as a godmother, considering your young age… so now you have the answer." We both burst out laughing.

I told her, "Just be aware that I will spoil him or her rotten."

She wasn't even pregnant yet, and we already talking about being some godmother and baby clothes. I knew she was 100% ready to be a mama. I asked her, "How is Rita taking this?"

"She's as excited as I am now, but also cautious because of the procedure and the 9 months that follows. But she's looking forward to raising a child, *our child*."

We left it at that. I told her I would see her next Thursday around 7:30 am, before they took her away for the preparation. She agreed and said, "I'm so glad you can come because being a mom is the best thing for me and the only thing that's missing in my life. I hope I get pregnant right away. That's always a question mark, however, I am full of hope and convinced I will be. Because this baby is so wanted, it has to work. Thank you, my friend. See you next week."

CHAPTER 26

On Thursday, March 30, I drove to St. Vincent Hospital, where Rita and Marianne were waiting for the IVF procedure. I joined them on the 3rd floor. Marianne was very nervous, and Rita was even more nervous then Marianne. Now we were three nervous people together. We held hands and chatted the time away. Bruno and Daniel were already there, Marianne told me.

I thought this was a fine gesture they were doing to make their friends happy. Marianne had told them they would have the right to visit the baby any time they wanted. Daniel's gift was the gift of life for a lesbian woman who otherwise would not have had a baby.

His partner Bruno was a wonderful guy. There was no hesitation from him about helping his friends Marianne and Rita. As a regular girl, I had a lot of respect for both men. After all, they had "the gift of life" in them.

Rita and I had a few coffees, but Marianne was not allowed to have anything to drink. The nurse came to take Marianne on a stretcher into the OR. Rita and I blew her kisses and gave her the thumbs up. We knew it would take a while, so we decided to go for a bite to eat at a nearby tea room. We were hungry, but very nervous at the same time and talked constantly about Marianne and raising a child.

I was surprised how Rita was so involved in having a child after the original way she had reacted when Marianne told her she wanted a baby. But then again, love conquers all. Marianne was the woman she wanted to spend the rest of her life with, and she had accepted her wish. This was a no brainer.

Around 10:30 we walked back to the hospital. Whether Marianne was back or not, we wanted to be there waiting patiently for her. She was told she could go home after the procedure, but had to rest and take it easy.

I had taken the whole day off work to stay with both and cook for them if Rita allowed me. We had been told that IVF involved a large amount of emotional energy and stress, therefore Marianne had to take it easy and stay in bed, and Rita had better behave and pamper her. I had no doubt that she would.

It was almost noon when the nurse wheeled Marianne back into the room. She was a bit groggy, but wide awake and smiling. We hugged her and squeezed her tight. She said, "All done. However, I have to stay another hour or so. Is it okay for you guys to stick around?"

"Well, of course," we both replied. "Where would we go? To the disco?" We all laughed out loud.

Bruno and Daniel came into the room and hugged Marianne first; Rita and I came next. They both looked radiant. As if *they* were going to have that baby… We chatted until the nurse came and told Marianne she could leave. But she insisted Marianne had to lie down in bed or on a sofa. There could be no chores – just plain rest. We all promised she would not be allowed to lift a finger. The nurse had a big smile and said, "We will see you next week for blood work and an ultrasound. I will bring you the appointment note in a few minutes."

CHAPTER 27

We all drove back home to Rita's house. It was around 5 pm. Bruno and Daniel left for work and kissed everyone goodbye. Marianne had been given the time and day to be back at the hospital for a check-up, ultrasound, and blood work. When we arrived, I took the initiative to order food for all of us. Rita and I were too exhausted to cook. We were all very hungry. Chinese food was the best and quickest way to have something delivered. Marianne lay down on one of the three-seat couches. We told her not to lift a finger, or else…no food.

She was so excited and chatted away like a runaway train. I ordered the food right away. It arrived 20 minutes later. The three of us were starved by now. We ate, not saying a word for the first 10 minutes, until we got the first hunger feelings under control. We toasted with a glass of wine. Only half a glass for the mama to be…but Rita and I took a full-to-the-rim glass and cheered to the happiness that was about to come. It was a good feeling seeing them happy and full of expectations.

A few hours later, Marianne got cramps in her abdomen and had to take a painkiller. The hospital had warned her that could happen. Marianne said, "I don't care about the pain. All I want is to be pregnant. Maybe it's happening now…or it's the Chinese food." We all laughed at her jokes. However, it was time for her to go to bed and rest. And me too. I had to work the next day starting at 11 am, and I felt exhausted from all the commotion. I hugged them both and kissed them goodnight. I told them I would be in touch the next day after work to check on my friend.

When I got home, I sunk into my recliner and poured a glass of wine in one of my crystal wine glasses as a nightcap. I was overwhelmed, but happy at the same time. Wonderful things were on the way, and I had the privilege of being a godmother for a baby that was in the making. *How crazy is that?* I wondered. I'm not that religious, but I prayed that night for Marianne and that the IVF procedure would be successful. Time would tell. I could not wait for the results of the ultrasound. I fell asleep as soon as my head hit the pillow.

My alarm sounded too fast the next morning. I wasn't ready to get out of bed. I lingered around in bed thinking about Marianne. In a way, we as woman have it in us to become a mother one way or another, whether through IVF or the *normal* way. When the time and instinct kick in, we are ready. That's why woman are amazing creatures. We can give life, when we are ready for it. IVF might cost a fortune, but if we wanted something badly enough we would go to the end of the world to get it.

"Okay Chantal," I said to myself. "It's time to get up and go to work." I had had dreams about babies and pregnancies. Enough now. A quick shower would wake me up and bring me back to reality. I've never sung in the shower but this time I felt like singing like Maria Callas.

When I arrived at work, time flew by. The restaurant was starting to fill up for lunch and then slowed down around 2:30 pm. Around 5 pm, it was the same scenario – hungry people coming from work or having a dinner date. My colleague took over from me at 7 pm.

I was happy I could leave. I rushed home and called my friend. Marianne picked up. I said, "Hey Mama-to-be, how are you doing?"

She laughed and said, "I'm fine. I slept all night and feel good." That was music to my ears. How one could be so preoccupied with a friend who had just had a procedure done to become pregnant? I guess she was my real friend, or like I said before, like a sister I never had.

I asked, "Yes, Rita had to go to work for a few hours till nine. You want to come over?"

"Sure thing, "I said. "I'll be there in 15 minutes. See you soon."

I jumped in my car and took off. I grabbed two sandwiches on the way to make sure Marianne did not have to make me dinner like she used to do. I also stopped by the florist and bought some nice orchids for my sister…

I did not even have to ring the doorbell. She opened the door when she heard my car on the driveway. She opened her arms and hugged me like there was no tomorrow. I presented her with the orchids. She started crying and said, "Chantal, you did not have to do this. Yes, I know we are all excited, and you mean well, but until I have a confirmation that I'm pregnant, please don't spend your money on flowers. By the way, they are gorgeous. I will take good care of them. Thank you, my friend."

She poured me a glass of my favourite wine and a glass of water for her. I smiled and said, "Hey, that's not like you."

She replied, "Well, I just want to be careful with the intake of alcohol. I don't want to make my baby in the making…tipsy." We both burst out laughing like teenagers. I could see Marianne was very happy from the way we chatted about the pregnancy and the follow-up she had to do in a few weeks to find out if the procedure had worked and she was truly pregnant. It was hard to wait. Time could not go fast enough.

I stayed for one hour and then headed back home. My thoughts flew wildly. *What about me having a baby one day?* I had an internal dialogue for a few minutes. I had to find the right man first, and I knew they were hard to find for someone as picky as me.

CHAPTER 28

The weeks went by and finally Marianne's appointment day arrived. I had spoken with her on the phone several times, and it seemed like her body was in a pregnancy mode. She could tell the difference. She had an upset stomach and was tired without doing too much of her daily chores. She said she had a good appetite and just hoped that these were the signs a baby was in the making.

The appointment was at the hospital at 3 pm. I told her I would be there. My co-worker would take over for me for a few hours, and I would go back after we had confirmation of her being pregnant or …not. "Did that sound good?"

"Yes please, Chantal. I would like for you to be there as well as Rita. I'm so nervous now that I can hardly breathe. I told her you must do just that – breathing – and not to worry because everything would be all right.

By 2 pm, the restaurant slowed down, and my partner took over from me. I told her I had an important appointment I could not miss. I would be back around 5 pm for the next rush of hungry customers.

I drove to St. Vincent Hospital a little too fast and was caught by a police officer. He made me stop and asked what the hurry was while I gave him my papers. *Should I tell him the truth?* I thought. *Yes, I had no other excuse.*

He saw my face turn all red when I told him that my friend was at the hospital to find out if she was pregnant, after having done IVF 5 or 6 weeks earlier. There I said it. I looked at him sheepishly. He smiled and said, "Well that's a hell of a good reason for speeding like you did. I will give you just a warning for now, but from here on, you have to obey the city's speed limit until you are at the hospital, all right?"

He handed me the warning ticket and I drove off. My heart was racing way too fast. I arrived at the hospital at 2:45, just in time to see Marianne and Rita. I told them my story about the police officer, who understood why I was speeding. They both laughed. I was happy with just a warning ticket.

Marianne said, "Then how are you going to drive when I deliver the baby?"

"Ha!" I said. "I have all the time in the world to think about that. And I may stay over at Rita's house, so she can drive the both of us to see you and the baby…"

The nurse came in and wheeled Marianne away to the examination room, where the gynecologist was waiting for her. Two hours after the ultrasound, blood work, and vaginal examination, the gynecologist's assistant came and asked Rita to join Marianne in the doctor's office.

We looked at each other with a question mark on our faces. Rita followed the nurse into the doctor's office and shut the door behind them. Now, I was getting a bit nervous. After all, Rita was Marianne's partner. I wasn't needed in the conversation. I waited patiently till they both showed up all smiles. Marianne had a blush on both cheeks and was glowing. She ran into my arms, almost yelling: "Chantal, my friend, I'm pregnant! I'm going to have a baby." We all jumped up holding hands in the hallway of the hospital. Every nurse that walked by smiled; they knew and must have seen this joy before.

I asked Marianne if they were 100% sure. "What about the blood work? Usually it takes a few days before you have the results? Did they do it right away?"

She said, "Yes, they took the blood to the lab before they did the ultrasound. I got the confirmation after they tested the blood and all the other examinations were done."

"Wow," I whispered. "That's crazy good news. Just like you said, Marianne, it's got to work because this baby is so wanted, and there you have it. Let's celebrate and have a bite to eat. They both agreed. We had a quick lunch at a restaurant near the hospital. Marianne was all bubbly and hopping around like a baby rabbit. I had never seen her so happy.

I returned to work at 5 pm. I told those two soon-to-be parents I had a deal with my co-worker that I would return to work after my not-to-be missed appointment. I promised to call them in the morning. I hugged Marianne and told them both, "Congratulations! It's going to be an exciting future from this day forward."

I drove to work singing with joy. I was going to be a godmother. I couldn't believe it. My night shift went by like a whirlwind. When I got home, it didn't take me long to fall into a deep sleep, dreaming of children on a playground…

As soon as I woke up and had my coffee, I called my mom. She had to know the good news. She was entitled to know since I had told her about my friend living with a lesbian girl and wanted to have a baby. She was happy to hear that the difficult procedure Marianne had endured worked the first time.

My mom asked me, "And when do I become a grandma?"

I knew she would ask me that question. I said, "Patience Mother. My time will come, and you'll be the first to know it. I must find a nice guy first, and then I can start thinking about a baby, don't you agree? We both laughed. My mom was my best friend.

She said, "Of course, sweetie. I was just teasing you. Thanks for letting me know about Marianne. I'm very happy for her. Say hello and send her my best wishes, will you?"

"Sure Mom. Bye for now. Big hugs."

After I hung up the phone, I called Marianne. When she picked up, I said, "Good morning, Mama."

She laughed and said, "Hey there, Sis and Godmother-to-be. I blushed. Marianne calling me her sister was wonderful.

"So how are you doing, my friend?" I asked.

"Well, I have to go see my family doctor for the first few weeks, and from there on, I will be seen by the gynecologist until the baby is born. Chantal, I can't hardly wait until I am past three months and can feel the baby kicking."

"You have no choice but to be patient," I told her. "I only have to work from 11 am till 2 pm. Is it okay if I come by the house?"

"Of course!" she said.

CHAPTER 29

By 2:30 pm, I was at Marianne's house. There were the usual hugs and kisses at the entrance. She trembled from excitement and had the radiant glow of a mother-to-be. I silently envied her for the first time since I had met her. *Was this jealousy? Was I due to re-organize my life and find the man of my dreams?* I wondered.

We took a seat next to each other in the living room. She poured me an ice-cold Chardonnay and said, "You're done working anyway. You are allowed." We both giggled like we always did, when something unexpectedly stupid was said. Marianne had a half glass of Chardonnay. She said alcohol was allowed, but only in moderation. "So, I will obey for once with a sip. I can't have you drink alone, can I?" We made a toast, bumping the crystal glasses against each other and said, "To the next generation on the way…"

Marianne said, "I still have to bring the news to Daniel. But I feel like waiting until I'm almost 3 months, what do you think, Chantal?"

"That's up to you, Marianne. I would let him know if I were you. He has every right to be as happy as you are now. He also knows that the most critical months have to pass by before you can be sure it's all going as planned. So why not tell him? I am sure he's as nervous about the whole thing as you were two days ago and is waiting to hear from you. Why don't you try and call him now?"

"All right, you are right again as usual." She grabbed her personal telephone book, opened to the Ds, and dialled Daniel's number. I lay back, cozy in a chair, waiting to hear the conversation she was about to have with the father-to-be (incognito). After a few rings, Bruno answered. Marianne said, "Hi Bruno. It's Marianne. How are you both doing? Oh, that's good to hear. Bruno, I have news for you and Daniel, is he there?" I quickly told Marianne to put on the speaker phone.

Daniel and Bruno were on speaker phone too, so I could hear the conversation between them. "Hi, my sweet Marianne, what's the news? Is everything okay?"

Marianne said, "It couldn't be better, my dear friend. I am going to have a baby…I am pregnant."

There were a few seconds of silence and then laughter. Daniel said, "That's the best news of the day. I'm so happy for you. It's just wonderful. Only one try via IVF, and you're pregnant. That's unbelievable. Let's get together one evening and go over baby names." We all laughed. Daniel was as excited as the rest of us.

Marianne said, "Hold your horses, cowboy. We still have a long way to go before I feel it moving inside of me. However, you can still write down any name in a book boy or girl and the next time we see each other, we will compare what we have written and decide on the best names. Sounds good?"

"Yes, sure," he answered. "But let's get together anyway one of these weekends at our place and celebrate the good news."

"You can count on it," Marianne said. "And thank you, Daniel," she whispered. "I couldn't have done it without you."

He laughed and said, "No Marianne, the pleasure was all mine. I am very happy for you."

Marianne returned to her seat next to me and started crying, leaning against my shoulders. She said, "I am so happy and nervous at the same time. Is that normal?"

"Yes, Marianne. I am as excited as you are, and I'm not pregnant." We both cried and laughed at the same time while holding each other. *This was unreal*, I thought. *I met this girl one day at a disco, and the next thing I know, she's living with a lesbian woman and now she's having a baby with a wonderful gay man as the donor. How wonderful is that?*

Marianne got up and said, "I am calling my mother. She should know the truth now. I haven't told her that I live with a lesbian woman. She thinks I have a boyfriend and that I wanted a baby without being married to him."

I looked at her in disbelief and said, "Why did you tell her that?"

"I wasn't sure how my mom would take it," she answered. "But now that I am pregnant and she's about to become a grandmother, I have to tell her the real story. I'm so nervous, Chantal." I took the receiver and put it into her hand.

"Here, call your mother," I ordered in a way that she couldn't say no to. "Put it on speaker so I can hear her too."

Marianne dialled with trembling hands. I heard a woman's voice saying, "Hello."

"Hi Mom. It's me."

"Oh hello, honey, how are you doing?"

"Mom, I'm pregnant; I am going to have a baby." There was silence and then a scream of joy. "Really? Oh, my sweetheart, that's wonderful news. How far along are you?"

Marianne said, "Not far yet, but the test was positive, so I wanted to let you know. Also, Mom, I wasn't really honest with you about who the father would be." She sighed.

Her mom said, "No? And why is that?"

"Well, I always pretended I had a boyfriend, but in fact I have lived with a woman named Rita for many years. I left Enzo a long time ago." Her mom didn't say a word.

Marianne continued, saying she was happy and loved Rita. She said they had a good life together, and the baby was conceived via IVF with the help of a gay friend who donated his sperm, so she could have a baby. "A child was the only thing that was missing in my life, Mom."

Finally, her mother found her voice and said, "Well I had a feeling you were hiding something from me. I just couldn't pinpoint what it was until now. Sweetheart, don't worry. I am okay with your decisions. If you're happy, so am I. By the way I'm overjoyed. I'll be a grandmother in 7-8 months or so from now, right?"

"That's right, Mom."

I could hear a sigh of relief from Marianne's mouth. She looked briefly behind her; I gave her the thumbs up. Marianne continued, "Yes Mom, you can cuddle and spoil your grandbaby as much as you want." I could hear her mom sniffing. She must have had tears of joy rolling down her cheeks and a wet nose.

Marianne said, "I'll come by the house soon and introduce my partner Rita to you. Is that okay with you?" Her Mom agreed, and they hung up the phone.

Marianne fell into the chair. "I'm relieved," she said. "It's like I lost 50 kg off my shoulders. I can't wait to tell Rita."

I said, "You did the right thing, Marianne. Your Mom has the right to know what's going on in your life – but not the 'hot details', of course. Sooner or later, you had to tell her anyway, and this was the right timing. I could hear your mom was thrilled with the news."

"She such a good woman," Marianne said. "We are going to be closer than ever before. I can feel it."

Rita arrived from work soon afterwards. She hugged Marianne warmly and gave me a bear hug. I told them both I had to go, but Rita insisted I stay for a "happy hour" drink. She said, "You can't leave yet. I just arrived. Let's have a bite to eat and talk about the future."

Of course, she was right. It looked like I had only come to see Marianne and that wasn't fair. The table was set in no time with appetizers and the necessary wine. We chatted the night away. Marianne told Rita that her mother now knew about their relationship and was okay with it. She wanted them to go see her any time they wanted. Rita looked very relieved. Finally, Marianne's family was aware of them having a relationship.

I left at 11 pm with a good feeling. My friend was now overly happy with the baby that was on the way, but also her love life was back on track. I thought that was perfect and healthy for Marianne's future. Rita was more than overjoyed to become a parent.

CHAPTER 30

Life went back to normal for everyone involved. I had my weekends dancing the night away at the Blue Note. Marianne and Rita had a drink at the Destiny Club once and a while. They had to tell the good and unexpected news to their long-time friends. Everyone was excited to know Marianne was expecting a baby. The question they always heard was, "Who is the dad?" To their amusement, Marianne said, "Santa Claus came by the house one night and 'voila'."

That phrase created hilarious laughter at the bar. The owners showered them with free drinks, but Marianne always took a Virgin Mary no alcohol for her. She was adamant about not having alcohol until the baby arrived. She promised herself and everyone else who was listening.

Two months into her pregnancy, Marianne called me one day and said the gynecologist had examined her and told her everything looked great. This was fantastic news. She then invited me to join them at Bruno and Daniel's house for dinner in a week from now on a Sunday evening. "Would I be available?" she asked.

"I will make myself available," I told her. "I wouldn't want to miss that."

"Great, I will let them know you're coming too. I told them to have white wine in the fridge!" I laughed and said, "In that case, I'll be there for sure." That was a first for me to be invited to a gay couple's residence. However, Bruno and Daniel were no strangers to me, and they were both wonderful people. I was honoured to be invited as a guest. I knew they and Marianne had a lot to talk about, and I didn't want to miss out on the conversation.

My mother called me that week and inquired about Marianne's well being. I said, "It could not be better. She is more than 6 weeks, and everything looks great."

"Sweetie," she added, "will you let me know if it's a girl or a boy?"

"Of course, I will Mom. We still have a long way to go, but you'll be the first to know when it happens, okay?" She asked me to come over that weekend as she was making my favourite dish; my mother knew how to tempt me when it came to food. I agreed to see her Saturday around 4 pm. My hours at the restaurant ended at 3 pm.

Every other Saturday I was off in the afternoon. That Saturday was reserved for my mother and my favourite dish. I drove straight to my mom's house. She was happy to see me and couldn't wait to talk about Marianne. I felt that she was ready to be a grandmother too. I had a weird feeling of readiness, as well, and that I should be on the lookout for a guy to start a family with of my own. *I must go out more often and meet more people,* I thought. I felt I was too involved in Marianne's life and sometimes forgot about myself.

I drove back home late that night. I wanted to stay longer if possible. For some reason I can't explain, I didn't feel like going back to my apartment. I had nothing to go home to, except my TV set. Was Marianne's pregnancy desire contagious? I knew it influenced me, but the feeling I had was out of the ordinary. However, I wasn't ready to go on the hunt for a partner that night. When I arrived home, I poured a cognac in my favourite glass, turned on some jazz music, and relaxed before going to bed.

The week arrived when I had to be at Bruno and Daniel's house. I tried to look my best. I knew the guys had good taste in clothing and wanted to make an impression. As Marianne's best friend, showing off a little wouldn't hurt. I arrived at the address I was given by Marianne. It was an impressive, huge mansion, surrounded with a white picket fence. I could see Rita's car. Thank God, I wasn't the first one to arrive.

Daniel opened the massive front door at the first ring. He hugged me and welcomed me into his living room. It was raining, and he took my wet coat to dry in the closet in the hallway. Bruno and my friends were all waiting; I hugged each one and took a seat not far from Marianne. Daniel came back and asked me what I wanted to drink. Bruno stood up and while walking to the kitchen said, "I think Chantal would like a cool Chardonnay, right Chantal?"

I nodded yes and said, "You must have been briefed by someone," looking at Marianne with a naughty smile. The room filled with a loud roar of laughter.

Bruno came back with my glass full of chilled wine. We all sat around the sofas looking at each other and wondering who would bring up the pregnancy first. Well, I did. So I said, "Who has the most names written up if it's a boy or girl?" I had to break the ice somewhere.

Daniel went to one of his cabinets and took out a piece of paper. "Here, he said, "let's compare." Marianne grabbed a notebook out of her purse and threw it on the table. "Okay," she said, "let's see how many of the same names we have."

We all smiled and looked at the names on the paper. Marianne and Daniel came closer together on the sofa and spoke the names out loud. They had four of the boys' names they picked in common. Alain was the top choice, which means "handsome". They both high-fived. We all laughed hysterically about how they had the same thoughts if the baby happened to be a boy. Daniel said, "We will bring up the girls' names after dinner, okay guys?" Everyone agreed. They brought out some warm appetizers, which we greatly appreciated; to be honest, we were all famished.

The interior of Daniel and Bruno's house was impeccable. They both had good taste. In fact, I would say expensive taste. The furniture was mahogany wood; there were hardwood floors in the living and dining room; and an expensive Persian area rug surrounded the living room furniture. I peeked in the kitchen and saw it had marble floors surrounded with stainless steel appliances, which must have been imported from the USA or Italy. Even the bathroom had marble floors. I had to admit that Bruno and Daniel had an amazing, warmly decorated, beautiful interior. A few minutes later after all the chatting about baby names, Bruno invited us to the dinner table.

Daniel, who was the chef at home, brought out oven-baked fresh salmon with roasted potatoes sprinkled with rosemary, a homemade tartar sauce, and a mixed platter of vegetables simmered in butter and onion. This was accompanied by warm French baguette for those who liked a piece of bread, which we all did. It was all so perfect. *What is it with those gay guys?* I thought. *They are not only good-looking, but also good in the kitchen as well. I think I need to take a course in cooking if I want to have a family any time soon. Maybe Daniel could teach me...*

Marianne looked at me smiling and said, "Bruno and Daniel, this is the best prepared salmon I have ever tasted, not to mention the veggies."

We raised our glasses and toasted to them both, thanking them for the invitation. After this gourmet meal, we all took a seat in one of the sofas. Bruno was clearing the table and joined us soon afterwards.

Daniel said, "Marianne, when is the due date exactly?" We all looked at him. He was very interested in the date. "Well Daniel," she replied, "it's going to be around December, I guess. I had hoped it would be a Christmas baby, but I guess the baby will arrive when it's ready. We have no say in this, right?"

I thought: *That's right, girl. These months can't go fast enough for all involved.*

I broke up the conversation about the due date, and said, "So if it's a girl, what are the names?"

Marianne started laughing and said, "Well it's 'Alain' for a boy. We agreed, right Daniel?"

"Yes, that's agreed," he replied.

The girls' names were totally different for Daniel and Marianne. I heard Charlotte, Marie-Jane, and Nancy, but no one said, "Yes, that's it!" so we all decided to wait until Marianne was at least 3 months pregnant to talk about names for a girl.

The evening went by like a flash. After desert and a brandy, Rita and I wanted to go home, and so did Marianne. She was tired. I didn't blame her. After all, she was a mother-to-be; we were just celebrating the occasion. We hugged Daniel and Bruno, and I said I was honoured to have been their guest and would not hesitate to come back any time for Daniel's cooking. Daniel blushed and looked flattered.

Outside, I kissed Marianne and Rita goodnight, and promised to call them the following week.

CHAPTER 31

As soon as I got home, I fell into my favourite sofa. I couldn't stop thinking about what a wonderful evening we had at Bruno and Daniel's house. These were unbelievable people. I would bet one of them would want to adopt a baby if they were given a chance; they were such a loving couple. I knew "regular couples" that had nothing on the caring, loving way Bruno and Daniel behaved towards each other. It was beautiful to witness all this.

At work one morning, I was called in to the office. The boss wanted to see me. I felt uncomfortable. *What did he want from me?* When I entered his office in the back of the restaurant, he smiled and asked me to take a seat.

He looked me straight in the eyes and said, "Chantal, you are doing an excellent job; I get a lot of compliments about you from my clients." I blushed. I could feel my face becoming all red.

I answered, "Well thank you, Paul, that's great to hear."

He continued, "But that's not why you are here." I thought: *Oh no, here it comes. Is he firing me?* "I would like to make you assistant manager of my restaurant. What do you say?" I almost fainted. *What would I say to this offer?*

"Well Paul," I said, "that's an honour that I gladly accept." I quickly added, "Would my hours change?" I didn't care about the days.

He laughed and said, "A tiny bit maybe. Would that be a problem? As I recall you live alone don't you? That way you don't have to rush home to make dinner for a significant other, right?"

Oh my, he knew everything about me, and yes, he was right. I just had my TV set to go home to. "You're right, Paul, I do live alone, and no it wouldn't be a problem. However, I drive home to my family every chance I get to see my mom. And also, I have a good friend who is expecting a baby, and I want to be with her as much as I can. Besides living alone, that's my only pleasure I have for the time being."

Paul looked at me and reached for my hand. He said, "Chantal, now that's why I want you to be my assistant manager, because you give your all for people, whether it's in my restaurant, for your mom, or for a good friend that needs your help once and a while. That's who you are and why we love to have you here."

"By the way, what's your friend's name? *Oh please, why did he want to know?* I thought. I said, "Her name is Marianne. We have known each other for 5-6 years now. She's about four months pregnant, and we are all very excited about it."

Paul said, "I can imagine you are. Listen, I will make it easy on you if you need to be away unexpectedly. I'll make sure you can. I know I can rely on you to be back when it's rush hour as you always do. Do we have a deal? And by the way, you will be paid accordingly. Your salary will go up."

I stuttered, "Yes Paul. We have a deal. Thank you very much for your trust in me." I stood up and couldn't resist hugging him.

He squeezed me tight and said, "Thank you for accepting."

I couldn't wait to call my mom and tell her the good news. She was as happy as I was. She said, "You deserve it, sweetie. You're one of a kind." I promised her I would let her know when I would come by her house as soon as I could. *Then, you guessed it, I called Marianne.*

She picked up the phone and sounded not so lively as usual. I said hey what's wrong, are you ok? She answered; yes, I'm fine but bored. I said well we will change that, I'm coming over, is that ok. Do you want something? Yes, please bring me a few Éclairs; I have a craving for sweets. No problem I said, I'll bring a few I can use one too. I have a lot to talk about, see you soon.

I arrived at Marianne's place 20 minutes later. She had made coffee for the two of us. I hugged her and said, "Mama, I was offered the job as assistant manager this morning and I accepted." Marianne threw her arms around me and said, "Wow, that's wonderful news. Let's celebrate that!" She ripped open a box full of éclairs and stuffed one in her mouth and mine.

We laughed like schoolgirls, wiping away the chocolate around our lips. She said, "Tell me all about it. Did you get a raise? Are your days and hours changing as well?"

I said, "Yes and yes." Marianne looked at me with those blue eyes. I quickly said, "Paul and I made a deal. I can leave if there is an emergency, no problem. I also told him about you, my best friend. I told him you were 4 months pregnant, and I needed to see you often. He understood that and made no fuss about it. So, you see I have it all under control. I'm happy, Marianne. I get a raise and a promotion from hostess to assistant manager. I'm in heaven; I love my job and the owner Paul too.

We both had our coffee with the goodies that I had brought. I asked her, "Why are you bored? Don't you have things to do? Why don't you go and see your mom more often? She answered, "That's not enough to keep me busy. I can't wait to deliver my baby. Only then will I be satisfied."

"Well yes, but that's still about 5 months away. How are things with Rita, everything okay?"

"Oh yes, all is fine with us," she replied quietly. I wasn't so sure about her answer; however, I did not probe any further. Maybe she had a bad day like all of us can have.

CHAPTER 32

Once I arrived at home, I was ready for bed. What a wonderful evening I had. I was happy I met Marianne at the Blue Note that Saturday night so many years earlier and was still part of her life. I couldn't wait till Christmas, or even 2 months from now. Feeling the baby kicking against Marianne's belly was already enough for me. And it wasn't even my baby… "I'm going overboard," I whispered to myself.

Two weeks went by before I called Marianne. I just wanted to give them some space; after all, they had a lot to prepare. I called her one morning and asked how she was doing. Marianne was happy to hear my voice and said, "Chantal don't wait so long to come by or call, okay?"

I answered, "Is that what you have to say to me after two weeks?" She laughed and apologized. She said she was feeling great, and everything was going well with the pregnancy. I could hear the joy in her voice. She said Rita is back to working full time. Since I don't work anymore, somebody has to bring in the money, right?

I asked her. "Do you miss your job?"

"Are you nuts?" she replied. "I love being at home. I don't even think about my previous job. And if I were to think about it, I would think I was way overdue to quit. It gives me chills just thinking about it. Of course, it was good in those days, making a ton of money, but I know now that's not life. What I am experiencing now with Rita and having a baby soon will fulfill my life 100%."

I was stunned and happy the way she saw her life as it was today, so different than a few years back. I still saw the face of Enzo, her handsome guy, preparing our dinner one evening.

I wondered what he was up to. Did he meet another girl yet? Would she be as pretty as his Marianne? I guess I would go by the restaurant where he worked and find out. After all, he had invited me when we spoke last, and the food would be on the house.

Then Marianne continued and said, "I'm almost 4.5 months now and have a check-up next week. "Do you want to come? That way Rita doesn't have to take a day off work."

"For sure, I will come with you. Just let me know the day, and I'll arrange something with work and free myself for the rest of the day." I added, "We could go for lunch if the appointment is in the morning, what do you say?"

"Sure thing, Chantal. I'll call you when I have the details."

It was Thursday when Marianne called me. The appointment was Friday at 9:30 am, so I needed to pick her up around 9 am. I had told my boss earlier in the week I had to take a day off, but wasn't sure when. I told him it would be this coming Friday, as soon as I ended my conversation with my friend. Thank goodness, I worked for a wonderful boss. He also appreciated my hard work and always being on time on the job.

The next morning, I picked up Marianne. We drove to her appointment at the gynecologist's office near the hospital. On the way, she was all talk. I didn't interrupt; I knew she was very excited. We arrived at the doctor's office 10 minutes before the appointment. Marianne turned to me and said, "Chantal, do you realize what a good friend you are taking the day off especially for me? You have no idea how I appreciate what you're doing for Rita and me."

I waved my hand and said, "That's what friends are for. You would do the same for me, wouldn't you?"

"Yes, I would in a heartbeat," she answered while squeezing my hand.

The doctor's assistant came in the waiting room and guided Marianne inside. I thought what a good feeling it was to be appreciated not only by Marianne, but my boss as well, and I was loved unconditionally by my mom.

I grabbed a magazine to take my mind off all the stuff I was thinking about. After an hour, Marianne came back, all smiles. She said, "Full steam ahead from here on. Everything looks good. I only have to see him next month when I'm in my fifth month. He said by then I should feel some movement. Oh Chantal, I can't tell you how I am waiting for that moment."

"So am I," I said. "Let's have some lunch."

We ended up in an Italian restaurant close by the doctor's office. We both had a craving for Italian food. Of course, I wasn't pregnant, but still Italian food was our favourite. While munching on our ravioli with cheese sauce, I asked her if she ever heard from Enzo.

Marianne looked at me in a puzzled way and said, "Why do you ask?"

"I'm just wondering what became of him and if he ever contacted you in any way."

She said, "I heard he has another girlfriend he lives with, so I assume he's happy. Well good for him, right?"

I added, "Does he know you're expecting a baby? Did anyone tell him?"

She shook her shoulders and said, "Maybe he does. I for sure didn't tell him."

I just wanted some conversation, but I could tell she wasn't interested in talking about Enzo any longer, so I changed the subject.

I drove Marianne back home after our delicious meal. She invited me in to stay with her till Rita came home. I was more than willing to stay and chat some more. She was bored anyway. "Hey Chantal, would you like an espresso or anything else?" she asked me.

"Yes please, strong coffee that will keep me going."

We talked about the baby crib, and all the things she would buy soon. After her fifth month, she would start shopping. She just wanted to make sure the baby was well and kicking. I agreed, "You better be sure," but added quickly, "you'll be 5 months pregnant before you know it." We both giggled like in the good old days.

When Rita arrived, I stood up to leave the rest of the night to the two love birds. I hugged Rita and Marianne and said, "I'll be in touch soon." Rita thanked me for taking the day off for Marianne. "My pleasure," I told her.

I headed home; it was kind of late and I had to be at work by 9:30 am. I thought it was a good day. Marianne was very happy, and that's what I needed to see. The baby was growing, and all was well. What a good feeling that must be for my friend.

That same weekend after work, I went and got a few drinks at the Blue Note. I saw a lot of people I knew and had a good time with them. I needed to let some steam off and danced the night away.

The next day I was off work and drove to my mom's house. She knew I was coming and had prepared gourmet food as usual. She was happy to see me. My mother was always happy to see me. I just hoped she wouldn't ask me if I had a boyfriend. I did not make much time to find a good decent guy with which to spend my life. When was that going to happen? We went shopping and had a good Sunday. She never asked me anything about a guy; even Marianne didn't come up in our conversation. She just wanted to focus on us. I left it at that.

Time and life went by. There was the usual work and home stuff, and occasionally I called Marianne who was now in her sixth month. She told me to come over one day and feel the baby kicking against her belly. I would do that in a day or two, I told her. The following Wednesday afternoon I drove to Marianne's house.

I had called ahead. She opened the door and hugged me as if there was no tomorrow. She always did that if I hadn't seen her in a few weeks. I took a seat; she opened a bottle of Chardonnay without asking me if I wanted any and came back with a full glass of wine just for me. She took a seat close to me. I could see the baby bump starting to show. She started talking and said, "Watch when I talk fast and long enough, how the baby reacts to it." I was waiting patiently for that to happen. In the meantime, I sipped my wine and popped a piece of cheese in my mouth.

Not long after we started talking about furniture and baby stuff, I saw the baby kicking against Marianne's belly. That was so cute. Marianne took my hand quickly and said, "Feel here. He or she will do it again soon." I held my breath and hoped to feel the sensation. Not long after, I felt it moving. What a wonderful feeling this was. It was tearing me up, and I had to wipe away my tears from joy. Marianne and I hugged, laughed, and kissed each other. It's amazing how a baby can bring so much joy in one's life.

I asked her if she wanted to know what the gender would be. She said, "Yes, next month maybe we will ask if it's a boy or a girl. I'm not sure. I want to arrange the baby's room as soon as possible. Would you come with me to buy some stuff? Maybe Rita will come as well, but if it's during the week, it's going to be difficult for her."

I said, "Of course, I'll accompany the soon-to-be mama."

Another week went by, when Marianne called me at work. She asked me if I could take half the day off next week Tuesday. I said, "Sure, I'll advise my boss way ahead of time, so I'm sure there will be no problem." My boss was a good man; he understood when I asked him for half a day off work to help my pregnant friend, and it was approved in no time. I called Marianne and told her I would be there around noon next Tuesday. It would be fun to go shopping for baby stuff.

On Friday night, I had the urge to go to the club on my own. I did not say anything to Marianne about it. When I knocked on the famous door, Paula opened it and greeted me with a big smile. She said, "Hello stranger, long time, no see."

I blushed a bit and said, "I know it's been a while. I just felt like coming by to see everyone." She guided me in and closed the door behind me.

Denise and Patty waved at me from behind the bar. They invited me to sit close to them, and as usual, the first drink was on the house. "So," Patty said, "what brings you here by yourself?"

I smiled and said, "I just wanted to relax, and this is the place to do that." They both laughed and confirmed my comment. The place was packed. I liked it when it was a full house. That way, eyes were not only in my direction, and I felt I could relax more.

I ordered another drink, when a woman with amazing, long, red hair and green eyes came by me and said, "Are you Chantal, Marianne's best friend"

I nodded yes. She continued and asked me how far Marianne was into her pregnancy. I said Marianne was now 6.5 months pregnant, and soon we were about to go shopping for baby clothing. The woman then apologized and introduced herself and said, "Sorry I didn't tell you my name. I'm Marie-Jo and I know Rita and Marianne very well. She shook my hand. It felt warm and soft. She asked me if she could sit next to me and chat a bit. I nodded and said, "Yes, of course," and moved a chair closer by.

Marie-Jo was very well dressed and had manicured nails. I thought: *I hope she's not in the same business as Marianne was once*. I guessed she must have been in her mid-thirties. I asked her where she lived. "Oh, not so far away from the city," she said, "about 20 minutes from the club." She continued to say that she lived alone. On weekends she stayed at her parent's house, and she was an only child. She then asked me what my occupation was and if I lived alone or with someone. I told her I was an assistant manager at a restaurant, and I also lived alone.

I saw some glitter in her eyes when I told her that. She asked me if I wanted another drink. I accepted, and she ordered two drinks. Patty and Denise looked at me with a smirk on their faces, eyes rolling, as if they wanted to warn me to watch out for Marie-Jo. I ignored it and smiled at them both, reassuring them I had it under control.

CHAPTER 33

Marie-Jo and I chatted away, asking each other questions, mostly about the past. She was telling me all about her life, and I told her a little about my life. I was not about to tell her I was a straight girl, because why would a regular girl end up at a lesbian club? She was very pleasant to talk to. Then, out of the blue, she invited me for a slow dance. How could I refuse? I took her hand and we both wiggled our way to the crowded dance floor. *I did it before, so why not now?* I thought.

Once on the dance floor, she took the lead. She knew how to manoeuvre and lead me, holding me tight against her. I felt a shiver going through my body, but I couldn't tell why though. Was it the sexy sentimental song? Or was it Marie-Jo who had this effect on me? We danced cheek to cheek, and it felt good. She held me as if she was a guy, except for her long red hair and her curves… My hands became a bit sweaty, and I felt embarrassed. Thankfully, the music stopped not long afterwards.

We never spoke while dancing, as if we wanted to enjoy just clinging to each other's body. I looked at her and thanked her for the dance, as we both returned to our seats. I gulped my drink in one shot, excused myself, and headed to the bathroom.

I needed cold running water over my hands to cool off. *What's with me?* I thought. *Should I stay or leave the club?* Marie-Jo was sexy, gentle, and sweet. It wouldn't be difficult to fall for her. I just did not want to risk it.

I went back and told her I was about to leave. I was tired and had to work the next day. She looked disappointed and grabbed a piece of paper and wrote down her address and telephone number and slipped it into my hands.

She said, "Call me sometime, will you?" I was flabbergasted. She wanted to see me again outside the club I presumed… I nodded and said, "Yes I will, but I don't know when." She agreed, stood up, kissed me half on my lips, and squeezed me tight. I waved goodbye to the owners, looked at Marie-Jo, and said, "See you soon." I headed for the door where Paula was waiting for me. She asked me if I had a good time. I said, "Sure I did and rushed out the door, handing her a tip."

I headed home immediately. I took of my clothes quickly and took an almost cold shower. I was trembling from anxiety, but felt hot and wanted to make love to someone – but to whom? I should focus more on myself and find a good-looking man.

I knew I needed warmth and to be loved. I felt it while dancing with Marie-Jo. However, it had to be by a man. I had seen how a woman could be when she had a jealous fit, like Rita. Women can be sometimes as cruel as some men are towards their partners. Marianne went from being a straight girl to living with a lesbian woman, and she was in love no doubt about it. They both went through the same problems that a man would with a woman. I just wasn't ready. I fell asleep soon after.

The next morning was Saturday. I decided to call Marianne before I went to work. I knew Marianne and Rita would be home. Marianne picked up, and said, "Hey stranger."

I laughed and said, "Guess where I was last night."

She right away said, "The club."

I laughed hard and told her, "What is it with you? Do you have a crystal ball?"

"No, I don't have a crystal ball, but I feel like something is up."

Marianne said, "Do you have a crush on someone?"

I said, "No, but someone has a crush on me. That one dance did it for me. I had to get out of the club, or I don't know what would have happened."

"What's her name?" Marianne asked me.

I said, "Marie-Jo. Do you know her?"

"Oh yes, I know her," she replied. "You better be careful. She is from a wealthy family, an only child, very spoiled, and a womanizer… Does that say enough, Chantal?"

I was stunned to hear this, and said, "I had a feeling she was from a wealthy family the way she was dressed and because of her manicured nails and polite manners. She had me in her grip not long after we started dancing."

"Oh," Marianne said, "I'm not surprised. She knows how to flirt and make you feel good, plus she is a good dancer, don't you think."

"Yes, she is, and on top of it all, she gave me her address and phone number."

Now Marianne was laughing again and said, "Well it's up to you to contact her or not."

"I don't think so," I replied. Then Marianne asked me if I would like to come over for dinner the next day, Sunday, after work. "Sure, I'll come. I want to feel the baby kicking…and see you guys."

"Great we see you tomorrow."

I got dressed for work and jumped in my car. Paul was there as always. He greeted me as if I was a relative. I rearranged the tables and chairs where needed and made sure the menus were clean. These were now my job duties as assistant manager, and I loved every minute of it.

Pleasing the customers was my priority and making sure everything went smoothly during the peak hours. On Sundays, my shift was over at three in the afternoon. I did not bother to change clothes and went straight to Marianne and Rita's house. I didn't even have to ring the doorbell. Marianne had left it ajar. I just pushed on it and stepped right in. Marianne knew I would be tired and had a bottle of white wine ready in the fridge. They both hugged me when I entered the living room.

You could see Marianne's baby bump very clearly now. What a difference since I had last seen her. She looked a bit tired I told her. She nodded, "Yes I am and resting a lot. I don't want to lose this baby or have it before the due date, you know."

I agreed and said, "For sure you better rest when you need it." I turned towards Rita and asked her how she was keeping up with all Marianne was going through. She said, "Well I try to stay busy and come home as soon as I'm done work. I make dinner for both of us and massage Marianne's shoulders and back if she needs it. She usually likes it," she said smiling at her partner. She poured a glass of Chardonnay for me, and had one herself, while Marianne had a homemade fresh orange juice. We cheered holding the glasses high; I sipped the wine slowly because I was so hungry. I knew I would be tipsy in no time, and I still had to drive home. Marianne called me over to sit next to her.

She took my hand and held it against her belly. I felt a lot of moving around in there. I smiled and felt humbled to witness the development of this much wanted baby for my friend. Marianne said, "Sometimes at night it feels like a soccer match in there." That was hilarious.

Rita hollered, "Hey, are you all hungry?"

"Yes, yes," I replied and so was my friend. We tiptoed to the table, while I gently caressed Marianne's belly and thought: *It's magic that there's a baby in there who will be joining this crazy world soon.*

I took a seat across from Marianne to have a better look at her. I thought she looked not as great as usual; maybe it was the pregnancy. I asked her if she took vitamins. "Yes, of course," she said. "I eat well, but sometimes I feel dizzy. This will all be over when the baby is born, I'm sure."

Rita came in with the food – potatoes au gratin, veal Parmesan, and sautéed asparagus. I praised the chef as soon as the food reached the table. "Rita, you are a wonderful cook. It looks delicious, and I'm famished."

"Then go ahead and scoop as much on your plate as possible," she said, laughing. I piled the potatoes with the asparagus on my plate with a piece of the veal. I waited while everyone else got their food, then Rita filled my glass up with another round of wine – just in time to attack the food…

There was little conversation in the first few minutes. Everyone was busy eating, and it was as delicious as it looked when I saw it arriving on the table. Marianne was not eating as much as I would like to see a pregnant woman eat in her almost eighth month. But like she said, her dizziness would be all over after the baby was born. Maybe she just wasn't as hungry as I was. I was full quickly. The potatoes au gratin was very filling and rich, but oh so good.

When we were all done eating, we sat down in the sofa and chairs. Rita was cleaning the table. I could not help but talk about Mary-Jo. I asked Marianne how long she knew her. She said, "About 3–4 years. I've seen her with several girls, especially new ones, and maybe for her you were that new one."

I laughed and said, "Well I am not stepping into her web, and if she won't receive a call from me, she'll know, right? I just hope I don't see her again at the club."

Marianne said, "Well that's always a possibility, you know that."

Rita asked me if I wanted a dessert or coffee. I accepted a cappuccino. That would be my nightcap. She added a small glass of cognac next to the coffee.

I looked at her and smiled, Thanks Rita, that will make me sleep for sure." Marianne asked me if I wanted to go shopping with her on my next day off. Of course, I would, I told her. We decided to do that the following week. That would be fun; I loved baby clothes, so cute. By eleven, I was ready to drive home. I kissed Marianne, held her as tight as possible – with the baby bump, I had to be careful, and thanked Rita for the gourmet meal. I told her the two of them would be more than welcome to come to the restaurant where I worked to have either lunch or dinner on the house. I would arrange this with Paul, so he could deduct it from my paycheck. They both agreed to do that one of these days.

I came home exhausted. I did not have to count sheep… and fell asleep instantly.

On Monday morning, I called my mother. She was happy to hear from me and asked me how I was doing. "I'm okay, I guess," I told her. She then asked about my friend Marianne. I said, "She's doing well. She's going into her eighth month, and we are going shopping for baby clothes next week."

"Oh, that's fun," my mom said. "I remember shopping for you when I was pregnant." It was so long ago, cut she still thought about it. I knew my mom was very happy with her pregnancy of her second child – me.

I said, "Mom I have to let you go. I have to prepare for work."

"Sure sweetie, thank you for the call. You know I always like to hear from you. Have a nice day and come home for dinner soon."

"Sure thing, Mom. Love you!"

I quickly took a shower and headed to work. The customers were coming in around 11:30 and by 12:30 it was packed. I was doing my rounds, making sure the customers were satisfied and everything was going well, when all of a sudden, I saw Marie-Jo sitting at a table for two near the window.

I felt my blood pressure going up, but tried to keep my cool. I went over and said, "What a nice surprise seeing you here."

She smiled and said, "Thanks. I wanted to try out the food at this restaurant as everyone is raving about it. I'm glad you're working today."

I asked her how she knew where I was working. She told me one of the owners of "the club" had given her the name of the restaurant and then it wasn't difficult to find the address.

"So here I am. I was hoping to find you here, Chantal." She winked.

I said, "Well I hope you enjoy the food, but I have to attend to other customers. I will come back to chat a bit later." Then I left. My heart was pounding so hard I could feel it in my neck. *What on earth is she doing here? What does she want from me?* I remembered what Marianne had told me about her.

CHAPTER 34

Thank goodness, the restaurant was very busy. Never on a Monday was it that packed. I was lucky I had my hands full, so I didn't look at Marie-Jo if I could avoid it. But at a certain point, I had some customers sitting near the area of her table and could not ignore her, so I smiled at her.

It looked like she had all the time in the world and wasn't going anywhere soon. I'm sure she was waiting for me to finish my shift to invite me to her table and try to convince me to have a date. Anyway, that's the feeling I had.

About half hour later, the rush subsided. People were finishing their meals and asking for the bill. While I helped clean the tables with the waiters, I glanced over to Marie-Jo's table.

She had ordered a cappuccino and was sipping at it in slow motion. She looked gorgeous the way she sat there, straight up and classily dressed. Her long red hair, which covered half of her back, was so seductive. I had to turn my eyes away because I had this strange feeling coming over me. Was it lust or the need to check out what it would be like to be with a woman? I just couldn't get my head around it. I needed to call Marianne and tell her about these feelings as soon as I got off work.

All the tables were cleaned and set for new customers. I didn't wait for Marie-Jo's invite and headed over to her table. I grabbed the chair in front of her and looked into her green eyes. I asked her what she was doing this afternoon and if she worked. She said, "I work for my father's business as an accountant, taking care of billing and making sure everyone pays on time. That's a responsible job isn't it? However, I can take off when I want. That's the beauty of working for a parent."

"So, tell me, Chantal, what are you doing after work?"

I said, "Well I'm off at 3 and back at 5 pm for the evening shift. Why?"

"Maybe we could go for a drink at my place. That way, you can relax a bit and kick off your shoes. I'll prepare a bite to eat before you go back to work. Sound good?" I nodded.

I knew she would want me to be alone with her; I hesitated for a few seconds, but then I thought: *What can happen?* Plus, I would like to see where and how she lived anyway. I agreed and said, "Give me a few minutes. I have to go to my office to finish a few things. I'll be right back."

I rushed to my office and called Marianne. She picked up and I told her what I was planning on doing – that Marie-Jo had invited me to go with her to her apartment for a few hours, and I had agreed. "Should I go? What do you think?"

It was silent for a few seconds on the other end, then Marianne said, "Sure just do it. You will see what she's up to, and she knows you're not going to be there the whole night because you have to be back at work. You have nothing to lose. Check her out. If she's too pushy, you can always walk out and leave. It's the middle of the day, so you can take a taxi back. That is, if you don't have your own car."

She was right; I had nothing to lose. "Okay Marianne, thanks. I will keep you posted and see you next Tuesday for our shopping spree. By the way, how do you feel?"

"Some days I'm okay. Today is a good one," she answered. A bit more patience and it's all over, right?

"Call me when you're home tonight, will you Chantal?"

"Of course, my friend, I will." We hung up, and I walked towards Marie-Jo's table. She had paid the bill and was ready to go. It was almost 3 pm. I waved at Paul to say "see you later". My heart was racing wildly. What was I to expect?

I asked her whose car we were taking. She said, "Let's take mine; it's parked in front of the restaurant. I'll bring you back later." We both walked out the front door. I knew Paul was watching us and probably wondered who this red-haired woman was. Maybe I would tell him tomorrow that I have a new friend, nothing more than that.

Marie-Jo's car was a Mercedes Benz sport with silver-grey and black leather seats. It smelled like new when I stepped into the car. I whistled saying, "Wow, this is a nice car you have here, missy."

She smiled and said, "It's the company's car, and they pay for it." She smiled while looking at me in a naughty way.

"Well, that's great driving around in this high-end expensive car at the company's expense." We both laughed about it and drove off.

Her apartment was not that far, just a few blocks south. We didn't talk much on the way. It was a four-storey building that looked new, with lots of glass windows. She drove underground to her private parking spot. The door opened with the push of a button. I was still very excited and a bit worried at the same time.

What was I doing here? We got out of the car; she locked it with an automatic click of a button on her key chain. I followed her to the elevators. She smiled and said, "Don't worry, I won't hold you captive here, you know." *Just the words I wasn't ready to hear or think.*

I said, "I'm not worried, just curious to see your apartment and have a drink. After all, you invited me, so now I will see how you live as a bachelor."

The elevator stopped at the 5th floor – the roof top. This must be some sort of penthouse. The hallway was beautiful and spacious, with carpet runners all the way to the door. It was very quiet. Marie-Jo opened the door and took my hand to lead me inside. I felt unexplainably hot, sweaty and nauseous suddenly.

The furniture looked very expensive. She quickly asked me to take a seat anywhere I wanted. I took off my shoes out of politeness because it was immaculately clean everywhere I looked. I sank into one of the single chairs because that way she could not sit next to me. Yes, I did that on purpose. I knew I was in unknown territory and tried to be cautious as much as I could be.

CHAPTER 35

Marie-Jo took off her shoes as well; tiptoed around me and asked me what I wanted to drink. "Coffee please," I whispered.

She looked at me, shaking her head, saying, "Are you sure? I have some smoked salmon with capers and a French baguette, which calls for some white wine, doesn't it?"

I smiled and said, "Yes, it does. All right then, one glass won't hurt. But remember I still have to go to work later."

She laughed and disappeared in the kitchen. A few minutes later, she came back with a platter of smoked salmon and a crispy baguette. She fetched two glasses out of a mahogany curio cabinet that matched her dinner table and coffee tables. Then she went into the kitchen and brought out a bottle of Veuve Clicquot, a very expensive Champagne. She uncorked it in front of me without spilling any of it. I thought: *She's a pro. If I opened that bottle, I would have that bubbly expensive liquid all over me.*

She poured the champagne in each glass and toasted, holding her hand high. She said, "To us…to new friendship." She took a seat in the other chair opposite me. I took a sip and agreed, shaking my head in a confirming way, while smiling at her.

I was waiting for what would happen next. She invited me to grab some bread and salmon that was waiting for us on the coffee table in the middle of the two chairs. She was very calm and collected, as if she wanted just my company and to get to know me better. I reached for the food. By now I was hungry. After my morning shift, I had to eat and create some energy for 5 pm. She rolled up a few pieces of the salmon and said, "Do you have a boyfriend?"

I must have looked surprised. She quickly said, "Sorry, if you don't want to answer that. No problem, sweetie."

I said, "No, I don't have a boyfriend. I had one for 3 years, but he was always broke, so I ended my relationship with him. I can't do anything with a loser, can I?"

She agreed. "How long was that ago?"

I told her it was at least 5 years ago.

"Have you had anybody else as a lover since then?"

I was now a bit more cautious. She was interrogating me. Fishing to find out how long ago it was since I had a sexual relationship. I said, "No and I'm not looking to have one for now. I feel good being alone for a while."

She looked surprised at my answer. She then asked me what I was looking for at "the club". I said, "I like to go there to just relax. There are no men hanging around, trying to take me to bed. It's a way for me to relax, plus I like the owners." I took another sip from my glass and munched some more on the food, trying to change the subject.

However, Marie-Jo then said, "But you are very attractive. You know that, don't you? Not just to men but woman alike."

"Maybe," I said, but I must be attracted to either one of them too, don't you think?

"Yes, of course," she replied. Now I saw her blush a bit. Maybe she knew she was going too far in questioning me and took a step back.

She stood up and excused herself and went into the kitchen. She called me to come into her beautiful, fully equipped, modern kitchen. She said, "Would you like some coffee?"

"Yes, coffee would be great. Thank you." We had 45 minutes left before she would have to drive me back. I complimented her on her well-decorated interior and her good taste. She turned around and thanked me, kissing me quickly in a flash on the lips. I stepped back and smiled at her and said, "You're a naughty girl and quick as a whirlwind." She laughed.

As I walked back to my seat, she followed me with the coffee and cream on a tray. She took away the leftover salmon and bread and brought it to the kitchen. She was back in seconds. She looked at me with glowing eyes, and said, "Would you like to be my girl? Do you want me to pamper you like you've never been pampered before?"

I knew this was coming. Marianne had warned me. I laughed and said, "I don't mind being your friend and going out with you sometimes, but that's where it stops. I am a regular girl, as you know. However, my best friend lives with a lesbian woman and I love them both they are like family. And yes, I go to the club for woman only, but that's about it."

Marie-Jo looked at me in a state of "I don't believe you". I'm not a mind reader, but she must have thought there was a way to convince me to let go of my feelings and experience the love of a woman.

I was getting a bit uneasy and stood up, asking her where the bathroom was. She pointed to a door behind the entrance. I was glad I had a few minutes to myself and held my hands under cold running water. This was going too far. I had to find an excuse to return to work.

I walked back and asked her if she was ready to drive me back to work. She looked at me disappointedly, but stood up and said, "Sure thing, sweetie." We stepped into the elevator that brought us back to her car. Once inside, she turned her face towards me and hugged me, saying, "Thanks for letting me get to know you. I do want to be your friend, nothing more. Is that all right? I smiled and said, "Yes, that's all right with me."

She sat straight in her car seat and drove out of the parking lot. I had another 10 minutes to spare when I arrived and sat in my office, thinking about my adventure. She was well mannered, I had to admit, but straight to the point when it came to seduce someone. However, I was not about to embark in such a relationship. No thanks. I just would have to stay away from the club for a while.

CHAPTER 36

The next morning, I called Marianne. She was waiting to hear from me. I could tell when she picked up on the second ring. She asked me how it was with Marie-Jo. I explained my interaction with her and how the adrenaline had the upper hand at certain moments. She laughed and said, "I told you so, but in the end, she was courteous and drove you back to work without being overly pushy, didn't she?"

"Yes, I was surprised. I hope she doesn't come back to the restaurant any time soon.

"Marianne, I will come by tomorrow if you have nothing else to do. Is that okay?"

"Sure, my friend, I'll be here. I have lots to tell you."

"Oh yes, anything special?" Now I needed to know.

She said Rita and I bought a property outside of Paris, in a place called Versailles. It's really beautiful and has a huge lot size."

Wow, now I couldn't wait till tomorrow to hear more. "That's fantastic," I replied. "See you tomorrow." I was very happy Marianne and Rita were buying a house; after all, they had saved up a lot of money to do this, and with the baby coming soon, that was wonderful. Actually, I never knew Rita had only been renting the house she lived in. But after all, I was renting a place as well.

The next day after work, I drove to Marianne's house. She welcomed me with open arms. "Have a seat, Chantal," she said, inviting me to sit close to her. The baby bump was now very visible. She looked great. A little pale, but that was normal, I guessed. I had to tell her everything about Marie-Jo; she giggled when I was asked about how long ago I had a boyfriend or made love. It was funny, but also kind of rude asking me when the last time I made love was!

Then Marianne told me she had a conversation with Daniel the other day about the baby's name. "We all agreed if it is a boy, we will name him 'Alain', and if it's a girl, we will name her 'Marissa'. Do you like it, Chantal?"

I said, "Yes, it's beautiful. It has both your and Rita's name in it, right?"

"Yes, that's right. We came up with the name out of the blue, and we instantly liked it."

So, did I. Now I really thought what a beautiful thing it was becoming a mother. She poured a glass of Chardonnay and handed it to me, saying, here's to the baby, whatever it may be, boy or girl, as long as it is healthy. That's all that matters." She held a glass of grape juice against mine.

We both took a sip and munched on some crackers and nuts. " Tell me about the house you both bought."

Marianne explained that the house had 4 bedrooms and 3 bathrooms; all around the house was a huge porch Victorian style. It had an orchard with apples and cherries. "You have to see it to believe it," she said.

"When can we see it?" I asked her.

"Well, why we don't go see it this Tuesday after we're done shopping?"

"That's a deal, Marianne." She grabbed my hand and held it against her belly. I felt him or her kicking wildly, probably from excitement and ready to see the world…

I left after an hour and headed home. I was ready for a shower and to go to bed. I had a re-run of Marie-Jo's conversation. I guess I fell asleep with a smile on my face.

Tuesday arrived, and I was at Marianne's house at 9:30 am. The stores opened at 10. I drove us to several baby stores and bought a bunch of newborn clothing. Because Daniel and Marianne expressed the wish not to know the gender and keep it as a surprise, she went with neutral but vibrant colours. Mint green and yellow were her favourite. I sneaked in a few things while she wasn't looking. It needed to be a surprise somehow. We had lunch at a nearby restaurant and chatted away about the upcoming event, the baby…

We drove to the town of Versailles, taking the highway to get there faster. Traffic was horrible in the middle of the day. Once we were closer to the house, the roads were small and narrow. There were a lot of trees, flowers, and green bushes as far as the eye could see. It felt like another world, with tranquillity all around us. It was nothing like the hustle and bustle of Paris. This was the perfect place, where a child could grow up without the noise of cars and the smell of gasoline.

We arrived at the house. It was huge compared to Rita's rental house. The house was empty, but Marianne had the key to show me the inside. She opened the front door, and as I entered, my mouth fell open. "Wow!"

Marianne laughed and said, "Let me show you around." We walked to the wooden stairs towards the bedrooms. The master bedroom was enormous; she could even put the baby's crib at the other end of her room.

We walked arm in arm into all the rooms and bathrooms. It was so spacious. I told her they did a good thing buying this house and wished them a happy life far away from the crowd.

She said they were moving in 2 weeks. I said I would help them with the move. "An extra hand is always welcome." She added, "Thank you, Chantal."

Marianne explained how she wanted the baby's room. It would be painted in egg white or yellow. She had it all organized. The furniture was in storage, including a guest bedroom suite for me or her parents. This house was to be a paradise for all three of them. I was sure it would be. I was so happy for my friend and looking forward to the arrival of this wonderful baby – a donation from two generous people with big hearts.

Before we left, we strolled into the garden to inhale the pure air and gaze at the trees. The fruit was half eaten by the birds by now. But it was November; winter was on its way. So was Marianne's baby.

CHAPTER 37

On the way back home, Marianne asked me if I would be attending the birth of her baby on the due date. That was without question. "Of course," I said, "I'll be there."

"My parents will be there too and Daniel, Bruno, and Rita, of course," she said. I just want everybody around me when I deliver the baby. I mean in the waiting room. She smiled. She sounded a bit panicky, most likely because it was her first time. I reassured her we would all be there.

It was about 4–5 more weeks before Marianne's baby would enter the world. I was so excited to know if it was a boy or girl. I couldn't wait. I still don't know why she was not curious to know the gender. But then again having a healthy baby was her only wish.

Two weeks later, on Saturday, November 20, I took the day off to help Marianne and Rita move to their new home. The moving truck was ready to be loaded. I stuffed my car with their personal belongings, like jewellery and papers. The boys were done loading and on their way to the house. I left the passenger's seat free for Marianne. Rita had her car full of stuff too. She wanted to make sure she had all their belongings with her and agreed Marianne would ride with me.

After an hour of wading through the traffic, we finally arrived at the house. The moving company's truck and drivers were already waiting for us.

Rita showed the guys where they had to put the furniture. It took them 3 hours all together to empty the truck. Rita paid them, and they were on their way. We installed a chair for Marianne to relax in the living room, while we unpacked our personal cars with the rest. Once that was done, we closed the door behind us and high-fived. We were all exhausted but content. The fridge was already working and stuffed with cheese, snacks, and cold drinks. We made a few sandwiches and ate on the porch, while watching the birds. The weather was still mild for this time of the year.

We all smiled at each other, and I said, "You will be very happy here. I can feel it in my bones. Marianne, let's get that baby out soon, okay!"

We all laughed. She said, "Sure, it would be tomorrow if I had any say in this…"

I helped Rita set up the bed and arrange some furniture, so they could go to bed when ready. The unpacking was to be done by them. Marianne had all the time during the day. She would not be bored now. I promised I would stop by on my days off and help her if needed. I left around 6 pm. It was getting dark, and I didn't want to get lost. After all, I wasn't used to this area. We hugged each other, and I was on my way.

My mind was rolling around while driving. I hoped Marianne and Rita would be wonderful parents. I was sure Marianne would be, but Rita would have to adapt to having a child that would share the love of her life, her Marianne. Only time would tell.

When I arrived home, I thought a shower was all that was needed, no food or drink. Exhausted from the busy day, I fell asleep as soon as I hit my pillow.

The next day, I had to go to work for noon. I had arranged that with Paul. I called my mom and told her about the move and the baby that was due soon. She sounded very excited for Marianne. I told her I would stop by Monday on my day off. She agreed and said, "I can't wait to see you, my sweetie."

It wasn't busy that Sunday in the restaurant, but I didn't mind. I still felt a bit tired from the day before. I wondered what Marianne was doing besides unpacking their stuff. I was a bit jealous in a way; I would like to live around that area too; it was so serene. Maybe someday!

I called Rita at work to check how Marianne was doing. She told me all was good. However, she added Marianne was limited in doing things around the house and became tired quickly. "That's understandable," I said. "I will go and see her Monday morning before driving to Mom's house."

"Great," Rita answered. "She would like that I'm sure."

Monday came soon enough. I drove to Marianne's house early in the morning, just after the morning rush. Marianne welcomed me with open arms. Rita had told her I would be coming down.

"How are you doing, and how's the baby doing in this new house?" I asked jokingly.

Marianne smiled and said, "As good as can be I guess. I have a feeling the baby wants to come out any day!" I told her to take breaks while arranging the house and invited her to take a seat next to me on the sofa, while we had a coffee.

She said when she had seen the doctor last week, he thought the baby would arrive early in December according to the way it's positioned.

"That's wonderful," I replied. "That means 1–2 weeks from now?"

"I guess so, Chantal."

She had hired a painter to finish the walls in the baby room and had chosen creamy, neutral colours. We walked upstairs, where she showed me the baby's crib. I envisioned the baby in it already. I sighed and said, "I can't wait."

CHAPTER 38

I stayed at Marianne's home till 11 am and gave her a hand opening boxes, taking everything out, and placing it on the table. She would only have to bring it to wherever it belonged. We hugged each other. I promised to keep in touch every day. Since the telephone company had given her a new number, I didn't have to call Rita at work.

My mother was waiting anxiously for my arrival. White wine was on the menu this time. She said, "We have to celebrate the soon-to-be mother, right?"

"That's right, Mom." We chatted away and had a great meal as usual. It always felt good to be home.

Days went by, so did the due date. Marianne would soon deliver the baby. I called her every day. She was okay, she told me, however very tired by the end of the day. I said, "That will be all over very soon. Have a little patience. After all, it took you 9 months. A few more days won't make any difference." She laughed. I could hear her voice trembling, slightly.

She asked me if I had seen Marie-Jo at the restaurant again. "No, not yet," I replied, "which is okay by me."

On December 8, I got a call from Rita in the middle of the night. She had brought Marianne to the hospital. The contractions had started around 4 am she told me. I said, "I'll be there soon."

Rita said, "The doctor said not to panic. It could take a while, maybe hours, before the baby shows itself. Don't hurry, Chantal. If you're here by 7 am, that's okay." I quickly left a message for Paul that I would be unable to come to work that day. He was aware ahead of time that it could happen without warning that I wouldn't show up if my friend went into labour.

I stumbled out of bed right after our brief conversation. "Oh no, the baby is on its way," I screamed, while taking a quick shower. My heart was pounding wildly. I sped to the hospital around 6 am. Rita had called Daniel and Bruno. Their car was already on the parking lot when I arrived. Room 38, she had told me.

We were all allowed near Marianne's bedside to keep her company and calm. She was all red in the face. Daniel held her hand tenderly and whispered quietly for everyone to hear, "Welcome to this world, wonder baby. We are all here waiting for you. You are bringing tears of joy to everyone in the room…"

Marianne did not feel comfortable with all of us around her with every contraction. So, we left the room. Only Rita stayed while she had these painful episodes. The nurses were wonderful and brought us coffee and tea while we were in the waiting area. Daniel was very excited and chatted away, wondering about the baby's gender.

Marianne had intervals of contractions the whole morning. Her support group became very tired. I suggested having lunch at the hospital cafeteria. They all agreed. Rita had a quick lunch and headed back to Marianne's room. Daniel, Bruno, and I welcomed Rita and Marianne's mothers, who came to see us at the cafeteria. They both had developed a good relation over the last year. Having both of their daughters living together as a married couple, they couldn't do anything else than accept the situation. And now a grandchild was on the way, thanks to that good-looking guy Daniel. They were both on cloud nine…

We headed back to room 38 and split the group in two. The room was not that large. The grandmothers-to-be stayed with Marianne until the next interval of contractions. The doctor came by every 20 minutes to check on Marianne's status. He came back out around 2 pm with thumbs up. He said, "It won't be long now." A sigh of relief came over us. We were exhausted. I could only imagine how my friend who had to deliver the baby must feel.

At 1:30 pm, Marianne was wheeled out of the room. Finally, Marianne smiled, waving her hand. Now the adrenaline took the upper hand. We were all holding hands. Only Rita had access to the delivery room. At 3:25 pm, Rita came to see us all, and said, "It's a baby girl. She weighs 3,5kg. She's beautiful, and all went well. Marianne is very tired, but happy."

We all danced around, holding hands, kissed the daddy and congratulating him. Daniel was overjoyed. The grandmas were too. I could hardly wait to see my friend and her newborn baby girl, Marissa. I hugged Rita and said, "Marissa has two mamas. That's a privilege no one has."

She smiled and took a seat next to us saying, "I think I'm tired and good for a nap." No kidding. We were all tired. But it was worth it. The baby was finally here, and it was a girl. I had silently hoped for a girl.

After an hour, we walked into another room to see the new mom and her baby. Marianne looked pale. She had a lot of blood loss, Rita told us, but it was all normal, according to the doctor.

I kissed Marianne on her forehead. "Congratulations, my friend."

She smiled and said, "Thank you, Chantal. Now I can move on with my life." Everyone took turns to wish the new mother all the happiness she deserved.

Marissa was beautiful and had reasonably long dark hair. Even with the eyes still closed, I knew she would have blue eyes from Mommy and Daddy. She had everything a mother could wish for

December 8, 1979, was a day to remember. I couldn't wait to call my mother with the good news. Rita and the two grandmothers stayed with Marianne. Everyone else had left. I drove home, but before crawling into bed for a nap, I called my mom. She was very happy with the news and said, "I'll buy Marianne a gift for the baby. That's the least I can do. Just arrange it for me to see her when she's back home, all right?"

"For sure, Mom, I will. I'm going to rest now and talk to you later. Big hugs." I hung up the phone and fell into bed like a log.

The next day I called Marianne's room at the hospital. She picked up and said, "Hey Chantal, how are you doing?"

I said, "Well that's my question to you, my friend."

She answered, "I'm doing just fine – a little tired but happy. I breastfeed my baby. She is always hungry. She'll let me know when it's feeding time." We both laughed.

I asked her when she would return home. She said by the end of the week. "Will you come by and see us?"

"Of course, I will. Can my mom come along to see Marissa too?"

"Yes, she's welcome anytime."

"All right then. I will give you a call when we are ready to see you. Can't wait to hold Marissa," I added. "See you soon, Marianne."

I went to work, and Paul was clearly happy to see me. He said, "So boy or girl?"

I laughed and said, "A baby girl. Her name is Marissa."

"I hope you are not too tired from all the commotion," Paul said. I smiled. "No Paul, I slept 9 hours nonstop. I'm ready to serve our customers."

"That's my girl," he replied. I was very fortunate to have a boss like him.

That day flew by like a whirlwind. Some of the regulars were happy to see me, and of course, I had to tell them the good news and why I had been absent the day before.

CHAPTER 39

The weekend when Marianne took the newborn baby home, I asked for the Sunday off, which was granted. Paul knew I needed to be with my friend the first time she came home with Marissa. My mother came along as well. I arranged with Rita the time we would be there. "Early afternoon would be great," she said.

My mother was excited to see the newborn baby. She had several wrapped gifts with her, and I could see she was thrilled and ready to be a grandma. I could tell!

When we arrived, there were more cars in the driveway. The two grandmothers already were preparing food in the kitchen for the guests, and of course, Daniel and Bruno were also there and eager to hold the baby and hug her. Marianne looked still fragile but relaxed. She was quietly rocking in a chair while holding Marissa. We all took turns holding Marissa in our arms. She was so sweet, and what a beautiful baby she was, with lots of hair.

Marianne was glad to meet my mother. She thanked her for the gifts and said, "You have the most wonderful daughter, and I'm lucky she's my best friend."

My mom blushed and said, "I am very proud of her. Thank you for telling me this."

Daniel was very proud to have accomplished what was expected from him as a donor. "Who would have thought I had such good genes?" he said. We all laughed and praised him for helping Marianne to realize her dream. We all stood up and hugged him one by one. He was very humbled and turned all red in the face, while Bruno watched from the corner of the living room, feeling very proud of his partner.

The day went by quickly. We ate and drank like Vikings, or that's how it felt like. Rita did her best to make Marianne feel comfortable. I could see she would be a good mother too. She held Marissa often and laid her to rest in the crib, far away from the bubbly crowd, so Marianne could interact with her friends and have some downtime. She came to me and said, "Chantal, I've never felt so loved and good in my whole life, and you're a huge part of it." Then she hugged and kissed me.

In a way, I was very proud to have been a part of her life and everything that we encountered along the way. We had known each for almost 7 years. I told her, "I'm glad to have been in that portion of your life. Fate brought us together as close friends a long time ago." She agreed, smiling.

Everyone left the house slowly around 7 pm. We all said our goodbyes, kissed Marianne and Rita, and thanked them for their hospitality. I told Marianne I would call her during the week. I had to bring my mom back home first. On the way, my mother told me it was time I looked for a boyfriend and settled down. I knew she was going to rub it in my face. I smiled and said, "Yes Mom. I will soon."

Once a week, I called my friend to see how she was doing. She said she had to go to the doctors occasionally to have the baby vaccinated and have her weighed at the same time. She had gained weight, and that was a good sign. However, she added, "I stopped breastfeeding. I feel too tired after feeding Marissa. She's now on baby formula." Marissa was now one month old and more beautiful than ever, the proud mom told me.

Everything else was going well, she added. Rita was very protective of the baby and took good care of her. "That's a relief for you," I said.

"Yes, it is. I'm surprised that she is all over Marissa. I would have never thought she would have that motherly instinct. All is going well with us too, so I can't complain."

Time went by. The summer of 1980 was approaching. Marissa was now about 8 months old. I saw her growing like the lilies in their backyard. Every visit, she changed. Between Rita and Marianne, all was blooming as well. They were a loving pair of parents and lovers at the same time.

One morning early July, I had a call from Rita. She said Marianne hadn't felt well lately. Maybe it was fatigue, or maybe a lack of vitamins. She wasn't sure. She sent her to the doctor to have some blood work done and a complete physical. I told Rita to keep me posted on her health. "It's important to me." She said she would.

The next day I called Marianne and asked what troubled her. She said, "I have dizzy spells and abdominal pain in the lower part of my body that comes and go. I feel like I have a hangover, and I'm tired all the time. I don't know what the cause is. We will find out after the blood test comes back."

Five days later, Marianne called me with the results of the blood work and other tests they had done. She had been invited to the doctor's office together with Rita. They told her that her partner should be there to hear the results. My heart was now beating fast. I asked her, "What did he say, and why did Rita had to come with you?"

She now almost whispered and said, "I have ovarian cancer and it has spread to other organs." She started crying silently on the phone.

It was like my heart stopped for a moment. While my tears rolled down my cheeks, I told her I would come by and be with her right now. She said, "No, Chantal, please. Rita is with me. I need some time to digest what the doctor said. Maybe in a few days, if you could come, that would be appreciated."

"Of course," I said. "I'll call first before I come, all right?"

"Yes, that's good," she said. "I am not good company right now. You understand that, right?"

"Yes, Marianne. I understand. Take it easy, and go get another opinion from another doctor, just to make sure they are right or maybe wrong."

"I will," she murmured.

I hung up the phone and started bawling uncontrollably. I curled up on my sofa in a fetus position. *No, that can't be true. They made a mistake.* I fell asleep for a little while and woke up with tears sticking to my face.

I mumbled over and over, "Ovarian cancer, no way, she's too young. It must be a mistake. Please let it be a huge mistake. I don't want my dear friend to die." What would become of Marissa? Would Rita take care of her like Marianne would? All these questions and no answers.

I went to work, but I was not in the mood to enjoy my day. But customers didn't have to know how I was feeling, so I did my best not to show it. I told Paul, however, what the situation was with Marianne. He was devastated and said she should get a second opinion. "Yes, I think she will do that, but if it's true, what a horrible time to find out now that she's so happy with Marissa. I just can't believe it."

After work, I called my mother and told her what the findings were with Marianne. She could hardly speak, and told me I had to go see my friend to comfort her and make her see another doctor. "Yes Mom, I will. I'll keep you informed the next few days, okay."

I drove to Marianne's home without calling her first. I knew I took a chance of her not being there, but that didn't cross my mind. I needed to see her right now. I got to her house 45 minutes later. She was home and opened the door, hugging me while her tears dripped on my clothing. She whispered, "Thank you, Chantal, for coming. I need to be with someone, other than Rita. Rita must go to work, whether she likes it or not, and I don't want my mom to be here all the time, like she has been since she knows what is wrong with me.

I asked her what the next step was. She would see another cancer specialist next week, but she added, "I think it's too late. I can feel it. I'm weak and have no energy. Even to pick up Marissa is too much. I think this has been going on before I was pregnant, but then I blamed it on the pregnancy. I had felt I always had a full bladder and painful urination, but I thought that was normal when you're expecting a baby. I never told the doctor about it. That was my mistake."

I was horrified to hear her say all this. And yes, I had noticed she was pale in the face, but I never thought it would end up being cancer. If only she had told the doctor about her bladder issue, maybe they would have detected the cancer in its early stages. She said she had called Daniel and told him what the doctor had told her. He was devastated with the news and couldn't believe his ears. Her mother had a nervous breakdown. Everyone was in turmoil.

I stayed at Marianne's place till Rita came home from work. I had made some diner for all of us, so that we could relax and talk about the next steps and encourage Marianne not to be overly worried until they had a second look at her situation. *It was easier said than done.* Marianne held Marissa tight at feeding time; she was already feeding Marissa with baby formula, and introduced solid food slowly. Soon Marianne would be on chemo and taking medications. She had no choice in the matter. Nevertheless, she was happy she could hold Marissa close to her heart.

It was hard to leave, but I had to work the next day, so I had no choice. I hugged my friends and told Marianne not to give up, and whatever the outcome would be, I was there for her always.

The week Marianne had to see another specialist, I told Rita to call me with the results. I did not want to burden Marianne with having to tell me the outcome. As hard as it was for Rita, she would call me, she promised.

The day of Marianne's appointment I felt very restless. My mind was all over the place, and I was glad the day was over. I couldn't remember the last time I went to a disco or the club. There was no time for that now. My friend consumed all my free time, but she needed me, and I would never let her down.

First it was the IVF moments, then the waiting to see if she was pregnant, then the happiness when she was pregnant. Then there was the name searching and the get-together with Daniel and his partner Bruno at their house. There had been Marianne coming out of the closet to her mother and telling her she lived with a woman. After all that, there was the move to Versailles to their new home where the baby would grow up, among the apple and cherry trees, far away from the city.

What an adventure. In the meantime, I had forgotten myself, but it was all worth it. Looking back to when I first met Marianne at the Blue Note, her good-looking Italian boyfriend, her steaming nights with Rita afterwards, then her hope of becoming a mother, and now the devastating news we've got a few weeks ago was unreal. I hoped the news Rita would have soon for me would be better than expected.

Two days later, Rita called me in the evening. She asked me if I was sitting down. I told her, "Yes, what's up? What did the doctor say?"

"It's not good," she said. "They were right the first time. She has ovarian cancer. Chemo would be an option or surgery to remove some of the cancer, but it had already spread to other organs. Her chances of getting cured were slim.

It was good I sat down. I almost fainted. Palpitations set in, and I waited a few seconds before I could talk again. I asked Rita what Marianne had decided to do – chemo or surgery. Rita answered, "None of it. It can only prolong her life a little, plus she would be very sick from the chemo. Now she still will be with Marissa as much as she can, and she can get everything in order like her will etc..... She wants to be here as long as her body is functioning.

I whispered, "That makes sense, but I still can't believe it. How long did they say she has to live? Can they tell?"

"They can only guess," she said, depending how strong her body is, but they said 6–8 months with chemo. If she refuses it, then it would go faster. I sat stiff in my chair, crying silently, cramming my fingers into a fist. Rita continued and asked me to go see Marianne whenever I had the time. I would do so, I told her, and even take some time off work and stay over at their house.

I called Paul to give him the sad news. I told him I would like to take a week off, so I could be with my friend and help her with the baby and daily chores. He agreed and said, "Take your time and come back when you're ready."

I called my mom and told her the same thing; I would spend time at Marianne's house while she was digesting the horrible news that any woman dreaded. Mom was crying too, and said, "You stay with her as much as you can, Chantal. She will need your company more than ever."

I worked the weekend and took the following week off. I packed some clothing and drove to Marianne's house. She was happy to see me and hugged me longer than she usually did. It surprised me she did not cry as she took my bag with clothes from me and guided me to the guest bedroom. She said, "You will sleep like a baby here. There are no street noises, just birds that wake you in the morning." I nodded and smiled.

"Okay, let's go see Marissa," I said. We both went down the stairs; there she was in her baby bouncer chair, giggling as soon as she saw her mama and me. Marianne picked her up and handed her to me. Wow, she was heavy for an 8-month-old baby. I loved her pink cheeks and big blue eyes. I held her close to me and kissed her tenderly. What a joy. if only she knew what her mama had to go through. I was glad she was too young to understand, but I knew. What a tragedy. This was so wrong. Marianne was in the prime of her life, and this cancer would take her away from this precious little girl who she loved and wanted so dearly.

We sat down and chatted about life. I asked Marianne what plans she had made. She looked at me, shook her shoulders, and said there's not much I can do besides make up my will. Rita will adopt Marissa, and she will have her family name with my name hyphenated. I'll make sure Marissa has some money when she grows up for school, etc. I know Rita will be a good mom to her.

I can only prepare for the worst that has yet to come. I know where I want to be laid to rest; I've chosen the music and the invitations for the people that I want to be there.

While she was talking about this as if wasn't a big deal, I got goose bumps all over my body. Thank goodness, Marissa made it clear she was hungry and broke our conversation.

CHAPTER 40

While Marianne was feeding that little hungry mouth, I started to prepare food for dinner. I poured a glass of wine for myself and asked if Marianne could have one too.

She said, "Oh yes, I'll have one. Nothing will stop me from eating or drinking what I like. Soon Marissa will be on soft food only. It's already been introduced, she loves bananas and fruit salad is her favourite. I said, all right then here is your glass of wine." We toasted to... nothing. There was nothing to celebrate, only beautiful Marissa.

Marianne was acting very normal, but I could see the worry in her face. I tried to hide my worries and continued the preparation for dinner, so everything would be ready for when Rita got home. In the meantime, Marianne laid down on the sofa after the baby had a full belly and took her afternoon nap.

I sat next to my friend, holding her hand. We looked at each other and talked about the memories we shared, how we had met each other, and what a good friend she had in me. It didn't take long before we both started crying. I knelt on the floor and placed my head in her lap. We both had to let go of our emotions. This was it. The raw reality had set in, and it took a hold of us.

I thought this can't be true, and hoped silently she didn't have to suffer too long once the cancer put her into the hospital. Poor Marissa. Maybe she would not remember her mama. She was too young. Fortunately, Rita was a good mom too, and she would talk to Marissa about Marianne all the time, I was sure of that. But still, I would lose my best buddy, and there's nothing anyone could do about it. Life's a bitch. Some live to be 100, and some die young. It's not fair. Cancer has no age or mercy.

Rita arrived earlier than usual. She also had made a deal with her work to finish before the rush hour, so she could be home with her partner sooner. She hugged me and kissed Marianne while she was still lying down.

I said, "Don't move a muscle anyone, dinner will be ready in 15 minutes." Rita laughed and said, "Okay, hurry because I'm hungry." Marianne stood up and came into the kitchen. I waved her out and said, "No mama, you can't do anything here, unless you need a drink." She laughed and said, "Yes, that's why I'm here. You're the chef, so pour me some wine, please." I squeezed her arm, smiled, and filled up her glass.

We heard a little cry. Missy Marissa was awake, and Rita went to get her out of her crib. Marissa's smile when she came into the living room brightened us all up. What a doll. Marianne took over and hugged her little girl, bouncing her up and down on her knees. I took some pictures, and filmed 25 minutes on my 8mm camera, so that Marissa could see and hear her mama talking to her after Marianne was gone. I didn't want to miss this opportunity. I told Rita to sit next to Marianne and Marissa, and I snapped about 25-30 pictures, making sure I had the best of everything.

I returned back to the kitchen and yelled, "Take your seats at the table, please. That's an order." Laughter filled the dining room, and all the seats were taken. Even Marianne was hungry, and she said that doesn't happen often lately. But I had made spinach-filled, fresh ravioli with a light cheese sauce, and there was fresh, warm baguette as usual with Parmesan cheese to finish it off. I knew Marianne liked Italian food, so this was especially for her.

We all ate quietly, with the occasionally bubbly Marissa trying to speak baby language, which made all of us laugh. I had to say Marianne didn't look depressed. Maybe she could hide it well, but I was so worried and sad that I would lose her. There were no words to describe it. Plus knowing Rita had to deal with it all and the baby was just too much to handle. Just the sheer fact that no one knew when this cancer would start to wreck havoc on her body made it even worse.

When night fell, and little Marissa was in bed, we all sat around the table. Rita told me that they had organized the last day on earth for Marianne. I was stunned that she had brought that up while Marianne was sitting with us. However, Marianne was well aware of what to expect in her final hours whenever they would arrive. She said, "Actually it's better one can plan this. When you die suddenly, you have no say in how and where you will be buried. Don't you agree, Chantal?"

"Yes, I guess so," I replied, not knowing how to answer that. My arms and legs became numb when she said that. Poor Marianne. She had so much courage, as she hid the fear behind her beautiful face.

We ended the night talking about all the things they and Marianne had done over the years, while I took notes of our conversation (as I always had for the last few years). It felt good to talk about the good times of the past.

I stayed a full week, making sure there was food in the house and that Marianne did not have to go out. She did try to go out one time, but tired quickly. With Marissa in the baby car seat, it was too much for her to handle. I cooked when Rita came home and pampered Marianne and Marissa as much as I could.

I left back home with a heavy heart. It took a long time to let go of Marianne, when I stepped out the door. I whispered, "I'm here for you whenever you need me, okay?" She had tears in her eyes, and so did I. I kissed little Marissa on her cheeks and left. I was not in the mood to be a good driver, and I sped over the legal limit (again).

Anger took a hold of me, and I was home in no time. I cried uncontrollably till I fell asleep.

CHAPTER 41

I went to see Marianne every occasion I had during the weeks that followed. She never complained, but I knew from Rita she wasn't doing well. Three months later, Rita called me and said an ambulance had taken Marianne to the hospital. We all knew that when she refused chemo and surgery, the cancer could kill her more rapidly, and I think that time had come. Her liver and internal organs were failing, the doctor told Rita.

Rita called Marianne's mother and family and her own mom to come to the hospital, when they had the time. She also called Daniel and Bruno to tell them what was happening. We all got there quickly. Rita handed the baby to Daniel, who was in tears, as was everyone else. It was a nice gesture from Rita to hand Marissa to Daniel, after all he was her biological father.

We all had to wait an hour before we could see Marianne. She looked pale. She was asleep from the morphine. We all held hands and surrounded Marianne's bedside. I could hear prayers from everyone and sniffles. After about 30 minutes, she opened her eyes and smiled at all of us. She said, "Nice to see you all here. I know I don't look so good, but don't worry, I feel fine." That was an understatement. She said, "I don't know if I ever going back home, but I'll try hard because if I have to die, I want it to be in my home and not here."

We all agreed and said, "You're not going to die just yet. They will get you back on your feet, and we'll see you at your house, okay?"

The nurses came in and asked us to leave and return the next day. The whole gang went to a restaurant nearby the hospital. We talked about Marianne's courage, and the struggle she still had to endure. Her mother was devastated. She had a grandchild now, but would lose her daughter. This was hard for her and everyone else.

Rita agreed that Marissa would be taken care of like Marianne would have done. She said, "I love our child with all my heart." She would make sure Daniel and the grandmothers would see her as much as possible.

I hated our conversation. I knew this was about to happen at any given time. We were all prepared, but also extremely sad.

The next day, Rita could take Marianne home. She was given strong morphine medication for the pain. Marianne would vomit after eating food, but it was necessary she ate to keep her going. The medication had to be given any time she was in pain. I went to see her at home. She was in bed. She tried to stand, but I told her, "No, you stay in bed. I can lean over and hug you right here." We both smiled.

She told me she could feel her life ebb away slowly, but when the pain came up, she needed that morphine patch.

She said, "I'm so sorry I have to leave all the ones I love and my darling baby. I think my disease is a punishment or my destiny for having lived the reckless lifestyle I lived in my younger days. It was all about greed, and now when I have a life I dreamt about and a baby, this cancer takes me away. Do you think that's my punishment, Chantal?"

I reassured her, "No Marianne, cancer can happen to anyone. It has no mercy or age group. Don't ever think it's your punishment. Your dream of having a baby became reality, and you will live on through your daughter. Rita will be the best mother she can have, don't forget that. You will live on in all of us sweetie."

That was too much. Now we were bawling and hugging. She had lost a significant amount of weight. I could feel her bones through her nightgown. If only she knew how sorry I felt to lose her, but I kept myself strong enough not to show it. I brought her some healthy soup upstairs while Rita kept the baby busy. Marianne and I ate together on her bed. We chatted about the good old times – like her Mustang, which was such a beautiful car, and the surprise she had for me when she took me to the club for the first time.

We tried not to mention the disease she had. After we ate, she felt like taking a nap. I left her room and went downstairs to be with Marissa and her mom.

"How's she doing?" Rita asked me. She's tired and asleep. She did eat a little, so that's good. I took over the baby, so Rita could go and check on Marianne. When she came back, she said, "She's sleeping now. Oh Chantal, what a nightmare." I had never seen Rita crying as much as she was right in front of me at that moment. I consoled her, as if she was my other sister. I felt sorry for her. She was about to lose her partner and love of her life. It was a horrible, painful situation.

It was mid-September – the 13th to be exact – and a cool but sunny autumn day, when I got a call from Rita who told me Marianne had passed away in her sleep. We both cried on the phone.

We both had known the day would come, but still it was hard and earlier than expected. The only thing about it was that she died in her own bed at home like she had wanted. She was way too young. She was only 33 years old.

Marianne had lost so much weight that the funeral director and the family agreed not to leave the coffin open for the last goodbyes. We would keep her beautiful as she was in our hearts and minds.

The funeral was entirely planned by Marianne. The church was full of close friends. The owners from the Destiny Club and some of her closest friends were seated behind the families. I guessed over 100 people attended her funeral.

Bruno and Daniel were holding each other's hands, while their tears rolled freely. All Marianne's and Rita's relatives attended this very painful, sad event.

Little precious Marissa was carried in the arms of Rita, as they both walked towards the coffin of her mother covered with white lilies. She touched it with her tiny fingers and blew a kiss towards her mom's coffin. There was not a dry eye in church when she did that.

The music Marianne had chosen was from the 70's era. Mike and the Mechanics' "In the Living Years" was playing softly in the background while we all took our seats. This was followed by Edith Piaf's famous song, "Non Rien de Rien" ("No I don't regret anything"). Marianne wanted us to know she didn't regret anything through this song.

The song had strong, touching words that gave me goose bumps while thinking about my own parents, and especially my own father whom I had lost at an early age.

After the moving eulogy given by Rita and myself, there were tears and prayers. Bruno and Daniel were two of the six people who carried Marianne's white coffin from the funeral home into a white hearse limousine.

Rita told me afterwards that Marianne didn't want anything in black. It had to be white, so that's what Rita had arranged with the funeral director. Marianne burial place was chosen by her on a hill, where one could see the city lights of Paris and the famous Eiffel Tower. It was beautiful, but sad.

I trembled when Marianne's coffin was lowered into the vault at the resting place she had chosen. I held Rita's hand, squeezing it firm. We still could not believe she would never return to us. I saw Enzo in the distance behind a group of friends, wiping his tears. He looked very sad. I'm sure his heart was broken just like ours. After the burial ceremony by the priest, we all drove to the home of Rita and Marianne.

Every member of the family and close friends gathered together at Marianne and Rita's place to remember their loved one and best friend. We all had stories to tell about Marianne's life struggle and determination to get pregnant. I had the video ready to play, which showed a smiling Marianne around the house and in the garden, holding Marissa in her arms.

Everyone thanked me for taking these last memories of the woman who touched them all in a special way, including me…

Her mother and family would never know she had worked at Topaz.

I stayed in contact for a few more years with Rita and Marissa, who was now a two-year-old toddler, bubbly and beautiful like her mama. Rita took good care of her. She never fell in love again with another woman and devoted her life to her daughter.

I stumbled onto the love of my life and moved away from the city. I got married and eventually made my mom happy with her first grandchild, a girl whom I named Melissa-Mary-Anne…

MARIANNE'S DESTINY

Marianne would never see Marissa taking her first steps.
She would never see her graduate, have a boyfriend, or marry.
Goodbye my friend. We love and will remember you forever.
This book is dedicated to you Marianne, forever in our hearts.
Chantal, Rita, and Marissa

CPSIA information can be obtained
at www.ICGtesting.com
Printed in the USA
LVHW04s1451050618
579659LV00002B/365/P